A Dark Romance Christmas

Leanne Alyse

Copyright © 2025 by Leanne Alyse

All rights reserved.

No portion of this book may be reproduced in any form without written permission from the publisher or author, except as permitted by U.S. copyright law.

Trigger Warnings

This book is not appropriate for anyone under the age of eighteen! Reader discretion is advised.

If you would like to go in blind you can stop reading here. This is a dark rom com, with that comes discussion of sensitive topics as well as physical violence. Below is a list of trigger warnings as well as things to know about the book. I do not condone these characters' actions.

Trigger Warnings: poor representations of BDSM, non con/dub con, murder, arson, blackmail, cSA (not on page, not between main characters), discussion of suicide, knife play, Santa play, degredation, breath play, bondage

This book is a work of fiction and not based off real events. Any resemblance to people or events in real life is purely coincidental. Nor is this book meant to be an accurate representation of the real world. This is a fictional story, suspension of disbelief is recommended before opening the pages.

If you have any questions you can reach out to my email: <u>LeanneAlyseAuthor@gmail.com</u>

Your mental health matters <3

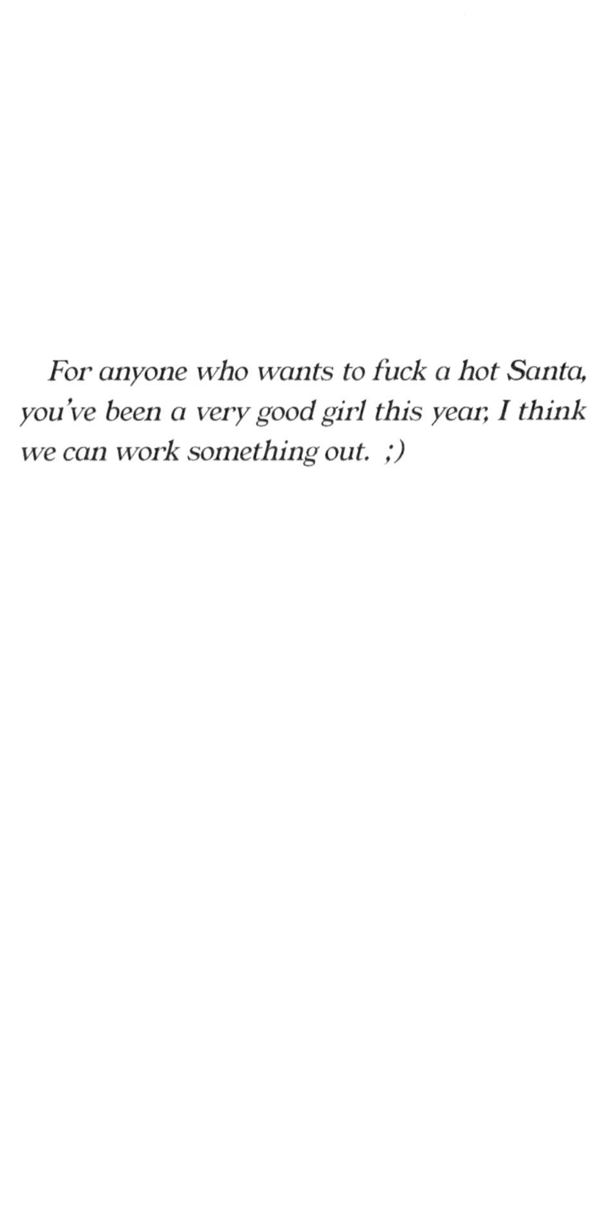

For anyone who wants to fuck a hot Santa, you've been a very good girl this year; I think we can work something out. ;)

Playlist

is it new years yet? – Sabrina Carpenter

Let It Snow – Sarah Reeves

Linus and Lucy – Vince Guaraldi Trio

Christmas Tree Farm – Taylor Swift

buy me presents – Sabrina Carpenter

Santa Baby – Ariana Grande, Liz Gillies

Baby It's Cold Outside – Idina Menzel, Michael Buble

A Nonsense Christmas – Sabrina Carpenter

Santa Tell Me – Naughty Version – Ariana Grande

santa doesn't know you like i do – Sabrina Carpenter

Chapter One

Quinn

"Quinn, come look, it's snowing!" My roommate, Madison, calls from the living room of our New York apartment.

I throw the last few pieces of clothes into my suitcase before shutting it. I head out of my bedroom and down the white hallway into our living room. The place is pristine with light gray colored couches and perfectly clear glass end tables. The high ceilings make the place feel spacious, especially for New York. Our TV crackles, set to a fake fireplace on YouTube to give us the ambiance, but sadly not the heat. Our place is always cold.

I walk up next to Madison standing at the floor to ceiling windows. I smile as I watch the soft flecks patter down onto the street below, intermittently rapping against the glass before melting away from the warmth. We are fairly high up in our building in one of the more posh parts of town so we have an amazing view of the city and on snowy nights like tonight, that's a blessing.

Madison is a best selling romance author and I'm an editor for a larger editing firm. We do well for ourselves, so we can more than afford the apartment. Honestly I'm suspicious that Madison could pay the rent on her own, but we have been roommates since college and I don't know if either one of us is ready to live alone yet.

I rest my hand on the glass enjoying the chill I'm immediately met with. "I love snow." I smile as the snowflakes fly past my vision.

Madison wraps her arm around me, her tan hand pulling me into her side. "I know you do." She smiles, brushing some of her black hair away from her face before leaning into me.

"I don't want to go back home." I sigh. "I want to spend Christmas here with you." I look down at her as we pull apart, before leaning against the window.

"You want to spend Christmas alone in the city, getting Chinese food from the restaurant down the street?" She asks with a laugh.

I shrug. "I wouldn't be alone. I'd have you."

"But in Vermont you'll have your family." Madison argues. "You'll have your dad. You haven't seen him since the funeral."

I start playing with my thumbs, my pale hands red from the cold weather and our freezing apartment. "I don't know what to talk to him about without my mom around." I mutter. "I love him, but it's just... I was always closer to my mom."

"Maybe look at this as an opportunity to get to know him better." Madison says, brushing some of my auburn curls out of my face. "And hell if it really goes terrible you can always text me and we can get you an early plane ticket home."

"Yes, because nothing says Christmas like taking the redeye back to New York on a moment's notice." I run a hand through my hair. "No, if I go, I have to stick around until after the holidays. It would hurt my dad and my sister if I left early."

Madison turns to head into our kitchen. "Maybe it won't be as bad as you think?" She asks, reaching up to our wine rack above our fridge and pulling out one of our nicer reds.

I scoff. "Come on, Mads, with my sister in law? I somehow doubt that." My sister's wife is not awful, but she is a handful, even more so now that she's pregnant. She's been helping my father with the bookstore since I moved out of town, and while I am grateful for that, she's been trying to change things.

My parents built that bookstore together. When my mother got sick and my father had to take a step back, Adriane started making the place her own. It lost that old school touch that made it so quaint and started to modernize. And while that modern touch has attracted new business, I just don't want The Maple Corner Bookshop to lose its roots.

Madison grabs two wine glasses out of one of the cabinets. "What did your therapist say about you needing to be more optimistic?" She asks, as she starts to fill the wine glasses.

"Hmmm..." I hum, coming to sit on one of the barstools at the kitchen island. "I think what she said was, 'stop telling Madison everything we talk about in our sessions.'"

Madison just rolls her eyes. "Whatever, you know you love me." She passes me the glass.

"And you love your dad too. So just try and make the most of it."

I swirl the wine and stare into my glass. "Yeah..." I mutter.

"That's not what's bugging you is it?" She leans back against the counter behind her before pushing herself up onto it. Her tone softens, "What's wrong?"

I chew on my lip and look up at her, knowing my blue gray eyes are watering right now. "It's the first Christmas without my mom." I sniffle, rubbing my nose trying to get control of myself. "She was always the one who put the holidays together and without her..." I trail off.

"It's not the same." Madison says solemnly, her light brown eyes soft with an understanding I wish she didn't feel. "I get it. The first Christmas without my parents was hard too."

"I'm sorry, Mads." I whisper.

She shakes her head. "Don't worry about me, Quinn." She promises. "Go enjoy the family you do have left. I'm sure it will be nice to see your sister. You two have always been close."

"That's true." My sister, Bridget is thirty four, only three years older than me. She is a detective for the local police station back home in Vermont. I always looked up to her. She was my guide through the world, until I decided I didn't want to stay in our home town.

"Focus on time with your sister." She encourages.

I nod, "Yeah." I say, wiping away the last of my tears.

Madison nods back firmly, "Now, on to more important matters, did you pack condoms?" She asks in a low whisper, leaning in and her flannel buttons split in the middle of her shirt.

I just about spit my wine all over my white sweater. "What!? I'm going home to see my family."

Madison shrugs, fixing her buttons. "You never know. Old high school sweethearts love to come back around for the holidays." She sing songs.

I scoff. "Mads, this isn't a Hallmark movie." I take a sip of my wine, the rich velvety flavor reminding me why I love the life I've built for myself here. "Besides, if one of us needs to get laid it's definitely you."

She puts her hand to her chest and gasps like she's offended before sighing. "Yeah... you're right."

"How long has it been? Since Dylan right?" I ask her.

Madison grumbles. "Don't fucking remind me. If I never see him again it will be too fucking soon." She leans back onto the cabinets behind her. "He redefines the term narcissist."

"You do have amazing taste in men." I muse sarcastically into my glass. She always likes guys who are classically handsome, but reckless as hell.

"Better than the dorks you pick." Madison counters. "At least the guys who fuck me are cool. Even if they are a little unhinged."

"I'll take dorky and stable over unhinged and cool any day."

Madison sighs. "Yeah well considering we are both single, I would say neither of us have had the best taste in men in the past."

I shrug. "Never know." I say. "Maybe some old high school sweetheart will come crawling out of the woodwork and sweep me off my feet when I'm in Vermont for the next two weeks."

"What happened to 'this isn't a Hallmark movie?'" She asks.

I take another sip of my wine. "Maybe I could use a little Hallmark movie in my life right about now."

"I just think that a mongoose should be a type of goose, not a long fuzzy squirrel." Madison shrugs, pulling my car towards the sign that says *Departures*.

"I get that, Mads, but it's not." I say.

She sighs. "Well at least some type of bird then." She argues, like I'm the committee on animal names and will somehow be able to change it. "And mongooses should be called... monsquirrels."

"One day, Mads, you'll solve all the world's problems." I chuckle.

She smiles broadly. "I sure think so!" Madison pulls up beside the door to the Spirit flights and puts the car in park. "Have a good flight!" She hugs me. "Don't forget your backpack."

I nod, hugging her back. "Thanks for driving, Mads." I go to get out of the car, but I hesitate.

"It's only two weeks, Quinn." She promises. "Then you'll be back here with me editing my next novel."

I huff a laugh. "Oh so you weren't going to send me that while I was gone?"

Madison blushes. "Maaayyybbbeee..." She stretches out the words. "I was going to try to hold off until you really started complaining about Adriane. Then I was going to send it as a distraction."

I chuckle and smile. "I like that plan, do that."

She salutes. "On it! And it's *full* of typos." She says like that's some kind of flex. "I know how much you love typos." She purrs, but she's right, I do love typos, catching them makes me feel like a god. No, your character didn't *gumble* because that's not a word.

I give her another hug and hear a car honking behind us wanting our drop off spot. "I gotta go. Send it whenever, Mads. I have nothing from work right now since I blocked this time off for the holidays."

"You're the best." She smiles.

I climb out of the car and grab my backpack and suitcase from the backseat before heading inside the terminal. I stare at the check in area for a second and do my best to remind myself that maybe it won't be as bad as I think.

I'm about to force my steps forward when my phone starts to ring. I assume it's Madison telling me I forgot something in the car, but when I pull it out of my pocket I see *Dad* on the top of the screen.

Taking a breath to steady myself, I answer the phone. "Hi dad." I smile so the greeting feels warm but the expression makes me more tired than I care to admit. It feels like masking and I just wish that wasn't the relationship we had.

"Quinn." He greets back, his smile also audible through the phone. "I was just checking to see if you were at the airport yet." His voice is cheerful, but it feels just as forced as mine.

"I just got to check in for the flight." I tell him.

"Good." He responds.

There is a silence that stretches between us and I'm tempted to ask him how he is doing, but I should get to check in for my flight... Am I just using that as an excuse? Probably.

"I'll see you in a few hours, dad."

"Okay." He says chipperly. "See you then." And then he hangs up.

I let out a sigh and head over to the kiosk to get my boarding pass. I type my confirmation code into the screen and get my suitcase checked in for the flight. Once that's done I start heading to TSA.

I feel guilty. I should have asked him how he was doing. I should have said something other than just blowing him off. I could have asked him about mom. I could have asked him about the book shop.

Waiting in line, I run a hand through my hair, playing anxiously with the strands. It's just that my sister has always been closer with my dad than I was. I don't know why that is, but they just seem to understand each other. I never had that.

As a teenager, my dad and I got into a lot of arguments about things I can't even remember now. My mom always said it was because I was stubborn like he is and a wild child like she was, a dangerous combination.

The older I got, my relationship with my dad improved, but when I moved away... he was pretty upset after that. College was one thing, choosing to go live in New York permanently meant being an hour flight or a six hour drive away at all times. They came to visit a lot when I first moved, but as I lived here longer it started to be only once in the summer and then when I came home for the holidays.

It's fine. Madison is right. It's only a couple weeks. Everything went smoothly last year. What could go wrong this year?

Chapter Two

Quinn

I look around outside of baggage claim for my dad's old truck, but I don't see it. It's been a few minutes... maybe I should call him? But then Adriane's SUV pulls up next to me, I find myself immediately thankful that I don't see Adriane actually in the car, just my sister Bridget.

She climbs out of the front seat and comes around the car to help me with my bags. "Hey, Quinn!" She smiles, her freckled face crinkling in joy. This airport is smaller and no one really cares if we take our time to load the car.

I stop her and give her a hug. "Hey, Bridget." Her heavy jacket is a puffy dark navy and squishes between us in the hug unlike my tan peacoat.

Her hair is a brighter shade of red than mine, but still her natural color. Her eyes are a soft blue gray too and now that we are adults and look about the same age, a lot of people mistake us for twins. "Good to see you." She pulls away after a second and loads my suitcase into the back of the blue SUV.

I shoulder off my backpack and throw it in beside the suitcase before hopping into the passenger seat. Once Bridget gets into the car I ask. "Where is dad? I thought he was picking me up."

She pulls out of the pick up area and starts to head towards the highway. "He wasn't feeling well." She says solemnly. "He's not been doing so great since mom passed."

I swallow a little, feeling some guilt for not being here to help Bridget with my dad. His health issues have been present for years, but she has mentioned intermittently that they have been getting worse since July. He had a heart attack a few years back and luckily they were able to save him, but his blood pressure has been iffy at best since.

"I think he's excited to see you though." Bridget amends. "He's been talking about it for almost a month. Plus I'm excited for you to get a chance to see the baby."

"Bridge, the baby is still in Adriane's belly. I won't be able to *see* anything." I correct her.

Bridget rolls her eyes. "Okay, Miss big shot editor, I'm excited for you to be around the baby. Give her a chance to get to know your voice since that's mostly how she's going to know you."

I sigh. "Bridge." I chide.

"I just wish you were around more." She says, the highway rolling passed us in the front window. "You can be an editor literally anywhere. All of your job is done online. You could move back home."

"New York is my home." I tell her. "I like it in the city. Everyone just minds their own business and I don't have to worry about things like Mrs. Johnson outing me to our parents."

Bridget scoffs. "That woman was such a bitch." She grumbles. "But she's dead now and I'm married to a smoking hot blonde so she can roll all the way over in her grave. The cunt."

"Do you talk like this around your baby?" I tease.

She flips me off. "No." She says seriously. "I tried but Adriane wouldn't let me. She heard me cuss once and told me if I did it again in front of the baby before she's fourteen that I would have to wash my mouth out with soap if I ever dreamed of getting to touch my wife again."

I laugh. "She's..."

"Don't." Bridget warns.

I shrug. "I was just going to say strict." A strict bitch, but I think if I said that to my sister she would smack me. For some reason my sister loves Adriane. They are happy together and as much as my sister in law isn't my favorite person it's more important that my sister is happy.

"How's Ashley and Caleb?" They are our cousin and her lawyer husband who live nearby. I don't love lawyers, but Caleb is okay enough. They are usually around for the holidays so I expect to see them while I'm here.

"Ash is great. She's working on baby number four, but she's not as far along as Adriane." Bridget says. "Caleb can't seem to learn how to wrap it." She chuckles.

I gag. "Lovely sentiment there, sis."

She waves me off. "Don't be such a prude. Maybe you're just bitter because you haven't gotten any in…" She sniffs the air, licks her finger and sticks it up before humming, "Five months, sis? Really?"

"I don't know how you do that." I bristle before conceding. "I am in a little bit of a dry spell, but that's just because I haven't been looking. I've been busy with work and I really don't need a guy complicating that right now."

"Mhm." My sister mutters.

We continue to chat throughout the rest of the drive until we pull off the highway and into the town that I grew up in. Most of the buildings are made of a red brick, many of them connected to each other or very close by. The ones that aren't red brick are a light brown or white like the church and city hall. Both of those buildings have tall steeples that stretch higher than all the other buildings but wouldn't even compare to the average height of one back in New York.

There are evergreens and leafless trees lining the road and sporadically growing around the town. We are basically in the middle of a forest so there is greenery everywhere even at this time of year. I do miss the falls here when the leaves all change colors, it's so beautiful.

The two lane road goes straight through town with crosswalks intermittently stretching across it and a couple stop lights, but most of the intersections are stop signs. There is a lake just a few blocks to the left, but it's likely iced over this time of year.

I get quiet as I feel like I'm being transported back in time. Back to high school when I had my first date at the diner down the street. Back to middle school when I was running around on the playground with my friends. Back to the moment I told them I was going to leave and tried to never look back. This feeling hits me every year, but for some reason, this time is different.

Bridget nudges my shoulder lightly. "You okay, Quinn?" She asks.

I shake my head like a dog trying to snap myself out of it, but it doesn't help. "Not really." I whisper, watching countless people go by, half of which I recognize, but their faces crease now in ways I hadn't noticed before, their hair is gray with the age that wasn't there last I was around.

I'm tempted to ask Bridget to take me back to the airport on the damned spot. I want to turn around, go home and eat Chinese food with Madison for the holidays and forget this small town ever existed except when I call home once every few weeks. But I can't do that. I'm already here and my family would be devastated if I just up and left. It would be like I truly have abandoned them.

Bridget rubs my shoulder gently. "It will be fine, Quinn." She promises. "You're over thinking it, I promise." I nod but she seems to sense my unease so she keeps going. "Everyone is excited to see you."

I just keep nodding, feeling like this town is going to swallow my soul whole. Maybe I can hide somewhere while I'm here and just tell everyone that I'm working. Is it too early to text Madison and ask her to send me her WIP?

My sister pulls the car into the driveway of the cabin that has always been our family home, the one that I grew up in, the one I ran from.

Boasting two stories, my childhood home is like something out of a lumberjack's wet dream. The outside of the house is all a warm wooden exterior with large windows placed periodically. The front deck is covered in snow this time of year, with tracks running through it as well as the lawn, both big and small foot prints, likely from my cousin's kids.

I see little heads popping out between the plaid curtains and recognize them to be Ashley's kids but which ones are which I don't know. I hop out of the car and head to the back of the SUV to grab my suitcase.

My sister waves me off. "I got your stuff." She says. "Go inside and see everyone."

I nod and climb the front steps up the deck, glad my heeled boots have some traction and that my leggings are fleece lined with how deep the snow is here. I'm surprised no one has shoveled the porch or the driveway.

I raise my hand to knock on the door, but Bridget calls from behind the car, "It's probably open!"

My hand hovers over the handle for a brief second before pushing down and opening the door. I'm met with a warm cinnamon apple smell and a rush of heat.

I walk inside calling out, "Hello?" Not seeing anyone in the family room off to the left.

The furniture is all a tan leather, two large couches and two smaller arm chairs by the fireplace in the corner. A large bearskin rug is in the middle of the room with a coffee table set a top it made from a wood colored similar to the cedar of the house itself. And of course a Christmas tree tucked into the corner for the holidays.

"In the kitchen!" Ashley calls and I hear the patter of little feet running towards me.

"AUNTIE QUINN!" One of the twins screams, but god help me I have no idea which one is which. I think they are five now, but I'm not entirely sure. All of Ashley's kids look a lot like Caleb, they all got the brown hair and brown eyes from him, but the curls from her.

"JACE! I WANTED TO SAY HI TO AUNT QUINN FIRST!" The other twin, who I can now identify as Alex, whines.

I hug them both. "Hi, guys." I smile warmly.

They hug me briefly before Alex goes running back into the kitchen. Jace grabs my hand and starts to drag me along as best he can, "Come on! You gotta try some of the pie cookies my mom made!"

I chuckle and follow behind him, letting my feet carry me through the familiar house. The kitchen is just as grand as every other room in the home. The dark marble counter and the warm wooden cabinets make up most of the space, but it opens into the dining room. The table in there can easily seat eight, usually for the holidays we have to bring in smaller folding tables to add onto the end so we can fit everyone.

My father is sitting at the table, his ginger hair is mostly gray with his age. He is in his seventies now, even if I want to forget that fact most days. It's always weird when your parents get older; a part of me wants to remember them as they were when I was a kid, young and full of energy, but that's just not how it is anymore.

His eyes are the same color as mine and my sisters but there is a tiredness behind them that I don't recognize in my own. The one thing that hasn't changed is his height. My father has always been tall.

My cousin looks the same as she always does, although she has a glow that makes her pregnancy obvious even if she isn't showing yet. She's younger than me and my sister, but all the women in my family tend to look the same. Ashley holds her current youngest, Amy on her hip, bouncing the two year old gently as she scoops cookies onto a tray.

"Hi Quinn!" She smiles. "I had extra apples so I decided to make apple pie cookies. Uncle Mitchell said he wouldn't mind me commandeering his kitchen for a little bit as long as I left him half." She chuckles.

"Quinn! I'm gonna put your stuff in the guest room! Then I'll be right down!" Bridget says as she makes her way up the stairs.

My dad groans as he moves to stand and make his way over to me. "Good to see you." He says, wrapping an arm around me quickly before pulling back away.

"Good to see you too." I nod, before heading over towards the kitchen and sitting at one of the barstools.

My dad sits down beside me at the center island and reaches across the counter to pluck a piece of cookie dough off the sheet. He eats it before Ashley has a chance to object and hums.

I chuckle and follow his lead grabbing the piece beside the one he took. Ashley goes to swat my hand away but I'm too fast. "That's really good, Ash." I say through a mouthful of apples and butter and sugar.

"Thanks." She grumbles, before scooping two more cookies onto the tray in the place of the ones we took.

"Where is Adriane?" I ask as my sister comes back down the stairs and into the kitchen.

"At the bookshop." She says, leaning back against the fridge. "She'll be there until six or so tonight and the rest of the week, but the store will be closed Christmas Eve and the day of too so you'll at least see her for the holidays."

I nod. "I was hoping to stop by there while I was here. I have a couple new signed copies of Madison's that I wanted to inventory."

"You don't need to inventory those." My sister chuckles. "I'll just take them. You know I love anything by A.M. Moonshine."

I chuckle back. "Bridge, I brought you copies too, it's why my bookbag and suitcase are so heavy."

"Yes!" She cheers. "I've been waiting for you to bring home her two new releases. I already have ebooks of them but I need those signed copies."

The boys run through the kitchen giggling before running back into the other room screaming something to the effect of, "YOU CAN'T CATCH ME!" And "YES, I CAN!"

Ashley and Bridget start talking about her pregnancy, but I'm not really listening. Ashley puts some more cookies in the oven, setting a timer on her phone when she does before turning back to Bridget.

I turn my attention to my dad and he smiles at me softly. A silence stretches between the two of us as I try to figure out what to say. After a minute of chewing on my lip I finally ask, "How are you?" And the question feels so stupid and basic that it makes me feel like I know nothing about him.

"Good." He nods, his eyes are focused on the cookies though that Ashley is pulling out of the oven. After another stretch of I don't know how long he asks back, "How are you?"

I shrug. "Good, just working a lot."

He nods again. "You've always been like me with that. I'm a workaholic too."

I debate what to talk about next, thinking I could try and launch into a discussion about my job, but I feel like he would be bored. I know he would listen politely, but that's not the same as being interested.

I could ask him if he's been working much at the bookshop. I could try and start a conversation with my sister and my cousin, jump into the baby discussion and try to be part of the family. But in the end, I don't.

I push off the barstool and head out of the kitchen. "I'm going to go unpack."

Chapter Three

Quinn

I'm not proud that I spent most of the night hiding in what was my old bedroom. I did message Madison for her book and she told me she was making me wait until Christmas since apparently she forgot to get me a present, she got me editing. It's fine, I can find other shit to do.

The guest room is still painted a soft blue, not because it's what my parents would have gone with to complement the house but rather because it was what I wanted growing up. The dresser is new and so is the bed, both made of a warm oak color; my childhood bed and dresser are too destroyed from years of use to be good for company, even if that company is usually just me.

There is a jack and jill bathroom that goes to my sister's old bedroom, but that has been turned into a craft room for my mom... at least it was. I don't know what's in that room now. I stare at the door with a curiosity I almost don't want to explore, but I do.

I pad across the white cold bathroom tiles and my hand rests gently on the handle of the old oak door. I shouldn't open it. I should leave my mother's memory to my father's privacy, but I don't.

The door creaks open on loud hinges desperately in need of some oil and I cringe at the sound. I peek inside and it's exactly as she had left it... I don't know what I was expecting. Everything broken in anger maybe? Or for it to be gone, cleared out because my father couldn't stand to look at it? But no. It's all just sitting there as if my mother might come back in at any moment and finish the painting set up on her easel.

The water color is beautiful, it's of an old bridge that I don't recognize. The blues and greens of the background blending and melding together perfectly to surround the center-piece. Something in it speaks to me and there is a sense of longing for a time long past, or maybe that's just me missing her. Either way, my mom always was a brilliant artist.

I run my fingers over the long dry canvas and pull them back up, almost expecting to see some kind of residue, but there is nothing. The canvas just stays as it is and so do I.

I need to get out of this house.

It's almost ten P.M. now and in a town this small that means almost everything is fucking closed. There is maybe a bar open, but drinking away my problems feels like a distinctly bad idea.

I head back into my room and catch sight of my suitcase, the books from Madison are sitting on top of it and while I was planning on taking them to the shop tomorrow I could go do it tonight.

My sister went home already to meet Adriane for dinner and my cousin and her kids left shortly after that too. It's just my dad and I in the house now and while I feel bad abandoning him to go catalogue books that could easily wait til after the holiday, I can't spend another minute in this house without my mom.

I fly across the hallway and forcibly slow myself down as I reach his bedroom door. I knock on it softly and hear, "Come in." From the other side.

"Can I borrow your keys? I need to get out of the house for a little while." I tell him honestly.

He doesn't question it. He doesn't try to stop me. He seems to understand where I'm coming from because he just says. "Yeah, on the hook near the front door downstairs. Try not to be back too late, the snow is starting to pick up and the roads will get slick."

I nod and head back into my bedroom without another word. I pack the books into an old duffle bag that was in the closet and toss on my peacoat and boots. I try to keep my footsteps gentle as I go down the stairs, but there is something desperate in them that I can't seem to hide.

Pulling the keys off the hook, I head out into the snowing winter of Vermont. The porch is just as covered in snow as it was earlier when I came in just with more footsteps trailing through it.

My dad's truck sits in the old driveway now frosted over and covered in tire tracks. His truck is covered in more snow than was just from today and it makes me wonder when the last time he drove it was.

I run my hand over the back seat handle, knowing he keeps a snowbrush back there but when I try to open it the door stays frozen shut. "Fuck." I mutter, pulling harder on the door trying to get it to work with me.

After a couple more good tugs it finally springs open just about whacking me in the damned face as it does. I go to grab the snow-brush, but it's not there. He always puts it back here in the winter.

Sighing, I resort to my only other option and start clearing off the windows with my coat. I didn't bring gloves so the best I can do is just swipe at the windows with my sleeve and hope that gets most of the snow off.

It works, kinda, and I get enough of it off that once I get in the car and get the heat on the rest should melt away. I climb into the cab and toss the duffle bag into the passenger seat. I try to start it but I hear a sputtering whine coming from the engine. "Oh, come on." I groan and try and turn the key again. It takes a try or two but eventually I turn it over and the engine starts. "Thank god." I mutter.

I turn the heat on full blast and it takes a few minutes but eventually the ice melts off the front windshield enough that I can wipe it away. I try to use the wipers and it takes a second before they start working, seeming to be stuck down to the windshield.

I back out of the driveway and onto the country road that leads into town. The visibility is low between the snow and the roads out here not having any streetlights until I get into the city. I do my best to drive slow, making the short trip exponentially longer, and after a solid twenty minutes instead of what should have been ten, I reach the bookstore.

I parallel park on the street which is fairly easy at this time of night because no one is out. I shut off the truck, not considering I may have an issue starting it again when I leave before grabbing the duffle bag and climbing out of the cab.

The street is deserted with nothing but snow and the glow of orange tinted street-lamps to light my path. The front door to the book store has a porch lamp illuminating it. The red brick building is connected to the one next to it and has an old wooden sign my father made above it that says, "The Maple

Corner Bookshop" in big red letters. It's on the corner of Maple Street, hence how it got its name. I watch the darkened store front for a moment before finding the golden key to it on my father's keychain right next to his house keys. His second home. My mother's second home.

I shoulder the duffle bag by the long strap and unlock the front door. The place immediately smells like worn leather, dark wood, and book pages. I inhale the nostalgia and find myself grateful that I didn't go to a bar. This is better than a drink.

I flip the light switches by the door and the place springs to life. Taking a few paces inside, I lock the door behind me, since technically the shop isn't actually open, I'm just visiting a little piece of my soul that I like to pretend doesn't exist.

The bookshelves are made of the same cedar that I recognize my parents' house to have been made from. There are shelves both lining the walls and in the middle of the space, creating rows for patrons to search through for their next great read.

My fingers run over the old shelves and this time, unlike with my mother's painting, I'm met with a soft dust. I thought they were doing okay... Why are the shelves covered in dust?

I carry the duffle bag up to the counter and am relieved to see that at least that isn't covered in dust. I walk quietly through the space and see some of the shelves are doing better than others. The romance section has open spaces and so does the fantasy. Maybe it's just certain genres that aren't selling.

I start to catalog the books, scanning them into the system and putting price tags on them for the store. I'm so focused on what I'm doing, that it takes me a second before I notice the smell of something burning.

"What the hell?" I set the books down and start trying to follow the scent. The lights flicker overhead before going out entirely. "Oh fuck." As I approach the back storeroom, I see it is entirely engulfed in flames. I'm about to reach into my pocket and call 911 but it is at that exact moment that I realize I didn't fucking bring my phone with me.

I rush over to the front counter, looking for where the store phone used to be and come up short with only a note listing the new phone number to the store and that if you need anything to call Adriane. They must have a cell-phone now instead of a landline. "Shit."

The door to the back store room bursts open, flames licking out of it as a man with short dark brown hair and a smattering of scruff comes walking through like he doesn't have a care in the world. He's holding a lighter and wearing a backpack that seems to be mostly empty now.

"Who the fuck are you!?" I shout at the man whose face immediately sours when he sees me. Something about him is familiar. Something in his facial structure is reminiscent of years past, but I can't put the pieces together in my panic.

His tall stature overshadows me as he backs me up into the corner of the desk. Hazel eyes shine back at me full of hunger and excitement as he stares into my being. He grabs me, his tan hand tight around my arm and before I really know what's happening there are hand-cuffs being slapped around my wrist.

"What the fuck?"

"Shame." He purrs. "I was hoping for no casualties." He leans into me. "Guess it was just wrong place wrong time, huh, firebug?"

"I'm the firebug!?" I shriek at him. "You're the one holding the lighter, pyro!" My rage boiling in my stomach.

He clicks the other side of the handcuffs into a loop in the counter.

"*No.*" I cry out struggling against the handcuffs as he takes a few steps back from me. The flames start to leave the supply room, coming to take away more of my parents' legacy.

The man who appears to be in his mid thirties, starts to set more fire starters around the shelves. He starts squirting what appears to be lighter fluid over the books, including the ones sitting right fucking next to me.

This man is going to leave me here to die... "*Please.*" I whimper out. "I'll do anything. Please don't do this. Please let me go."

"Begging is unbecoming, bug." He roars over the flames starting to lick their way through the stacks. He comes back around to me, wrestling against my restraints. "But let's talk about this, *anything.*"

I swallow hard immediately not liking the direction that this is going, but I stand firm on my word. "Anything." I repeat, stronger this time, projecting a confidence I absolutely don't feel.

"There is nothing I want from you." He shrugs.

I bristle, but counter. "If that were true, why are you standing so close to me?"

He chuckles like everything around us isn't actively going up in flames as we speak. "I can think of something, but a girl who reeks of city, like yourself, would never stoop to such levels."

I shake my head. "Try me." I push, taking a step into him as best I can with the cuffs, but getting caught.

The mystery man brushes some of my hair out of my face. "Yeah?" He purrs, his hand coming to snake around my body. His touch is warm and as much as I should I don't immediately cringe away. Something about that old familiarity makes him comfortable, even in this situation. He smells like smoke and I can't tell if that's because of the fire or because of him.

I look up into his eyes and nod. "Yeah."

He leans down to kiss me and I find myself kissing him right back. The adrenaline shooting through my system causing me to fucking forget everything except the man in front of me. But then he pulls away. "Maybe next time, bug."

The man pulls a cigarette out of his jacket pocket and lights it. He takes a few drags before shaking it at me and saying, "These things will kill you." And tossing the lit butt onto one of the shelves.

Chapter Four

Beckett

"*No!*" Quinn shrieks as I toss the cigarette. She drops to her knees and starts crying, but she might just be trying to get away from the smoke.

I spent weeks talking to this hacker I met trying to learn a bunch of bullshit to disable the nearby cameras but then I went to go see them in person and learned they were all just plug-ins. I unplugged them a week ago and no one has bothered to plug them back in.

People in this town are too trusting.

Not Quinn though. That's why she got out. She knows better. She knows how fucking toxic this town is and all the parasites in it. I find myself jealous of that most days. I couldn't leave for years because of my parents. I don't know why I don't leave now.

I watch the flames and feel at home, absorbing the warmth of the orange glow. The red tones lick around the edges and I want to reach out and touch the beauty I've created, but that's not really an option. Fire is a cruel mistress and I may love her, but she doesn't love me back.

Reminds me of someone else I know.

"Please." Quinn's voice is getting weak. I can tell she's getting light headed. "Please uncuff me." She begs.

I just shrug. "Sorry, firebug." I pull a mask up around my face to help combat the smoke, but I'm not in the bad part of the store like she is.

I will uncuff her, but not until she passes out. That way I can claim her memory is spotty when I carry her out of here. Easier to frame someone for a crime when they don't accurately remember what happened. Given the evidence I have against her isn't that strong, but as long as *she* believes I can reasonably pin this on her, she'll do what I want. At least, I hope she will.

I didn't know Quinn was going to be here tonight. I was planning to show up at her parents' house tomorrow morning with the accusations of her burning the shop down, but her being here so late and so randomly does make my case look a hell of a lot better.

Quinn takes a few gasping breaths as she starts coughing and I see her eyes grow heavy. I walk over to her and find the handcuff key in my pocket. Luckily I brought those, although if you would have asked my younger self I would have hoped to get her in handcuffs in a different way.

I had a crush on Quinn for longer than I can actually remember. She was always around my sister, Lila, when they were young and while her and I never spent that much time together, we spent enough for me to want her.

I guess some of those old feelings are still there considering I did kiss her. That was a bad idea. I've been furious at Quinn since the trial was over, I've never truly forgiven her for that, but this... this is definitely making me feel better.

Quinn slumps over and I uncuff her. I check her breathing and make sure she is still alive.

I'm not really trying to kill her, but hey, if the fire decides it's her time, who am I to stop it?

She is breathing so I guess the fire spared her, but her breaths are shallow. I pick her up in my arms and carry her out of the bookshop that will soon be nothing more than a pile of ash.

As I set her down on a bench across the street, I dial 911. I hadn't been planning to call this in, but now I need to get help for Quinn. I guess it won't spread to the other buildings now, which in theory is a good thing, but I was kinda excited for the bonfire. This town deserves to burn.

The operator picks up immediately, "911, what's your emergency?"

I force my voice to seem more surprised than I am. "I just saw a woman in a burning building. I'm a fire fighter locally and I managed to pull her out but I need the rest of the team to help put out the fire."

"What is your location?"

I rattle off the address quickly, putting my fingers to Quinn's neck again to check her pulse. It's steady enough, I find myself relieved in a way that I almost wish I wasn't. I really don't want to care about her, I'm trying very hard not to actually.

The 911 operator asks me a handful more questions before telling me she'll send someone right away. I can't help but feel like right away might have been faster if she would have sent someone when I gave her the address, but honestly, it's whatever. The longer she takes to dispatch my team the more I get to watch the fire burn.

I've always had a fascination with fire. This is the first time I was able to act on it. Usually my job is to destroy fire, not create it. I wish there was a job where you just set shit on fire all the fucking time. *That*, that is my dream job. Putting out fires at least allows me to be close to them, but most of my days aren't usually spent that way.

No, as fire chief I spend the majority of my time now either doing paperwork or helping with EMT calls. Very few fires actually take place in this area, most of the ones we do have are disappointing kitchen fires. Maybe I could move to California. They have forest fires that go on for days.

Either way, this is the biggest fire I've seen in my life and that means it's going to be the biggest fire any of my men have seen either. This is going to be a bitch to put out.

My attention shifts back and forth between checking that Quinn is alive and watching the orange flames lick up the bookshelves and devour the mess I've created. It's beautiful, almost as beautiful as Quinn.

Firetrucks start to arrive and when the first one does one of my men is passing me turnout gear. "Better suit up, boss." Albert says. He was the chief before me, but he stepped down when his wife started having health issues. He actually recommended me for the job. "It's going to be a long night."

He has no fucking idea.

Chapter Five

Quinn

The next thing I actively remember is someone carrying me from the burning wreckage of my parents' shop. I sit outside the shop on the ledge of an ambulance, drinking in the oxygen from the mask they strapped onto me.

Someone called the police but who, I have absolutely no idea because there was no one around when I came in. It could have been the mystery man, but I somehow find that hard to believe. One of the EMTs got my sister's number from me and they were able to call her. She rushed right out and has been sitting with me watching the firefighters soak our family's life work in our tears, very inefficient for putting out a fire.

And it's still not out... They have been trying for twenty minutes and the building next door started to catch on fire too because it got so bad. The flames lick at the sky without a care, the arsonist having done one hell of a job on the place.

"He left me for dead." I mutter.

"Who?" Bridget asks.

I shake my head. "I don't know."

"Quinn, the firefighters said that you were just passed out on the floor when they found you. There was no one else in the store." Bridget says in her soft voice, trying to calm me like I'm a raging bull.

"I know what I saw, Bridge." I'm trying not to shout and I keep my tone as serious as possible, but I'm too worked up and it's not happening.

She brushes some of the hair out of my face. "Quinn, you inhaled a lot of smoke. The paramedics are surprised you're even alive, let alone sitting up right."

"I'm fine!" I go to take the mask off to prove my point but when I do I start coughing.

"Ma'am, you need to keep that on." One of the paramedics says, coming over to put it back on my face forcibly since apparently I can't be trusted to do so on my own.

"I'm fine." I mutter through the mask, but I don't make another attempt to take it back off.

Bridget and I sit quietly, her arm wrapped around me as we watch the firefighters finally put out the store front. It's mostly rubble and ash now. Nothing left of the front sign or the shelves or even the door. It was all too flammable and when it went up, it went up in a blaze.

My sister turns to me, starting to sob softly into my shoulder. "I loved that book store." Bridget sniffles, her breathing becoming ragged as I pull her into me.

I shush her as best as I can through the oxygen mask. "It's going to be okay, Bridge." I promise, even though I don't know if that's true.

"How are we going to tell dad?" She shrieks into my soot covered coat. "Adriane doesn't have a job anymore. What about mom's paintings that were on the walls?"

I just keep repeating, "It's going to be okay, Bridge." Not even slightly feeling it as I watch one of the firefighters go through the place and start to assess the wreckage.

The yellow stripes on his uniform illuminate in the streetlights and his tall frame makes the ruins seem small by comparison. He looks through everything like he's trying to find something, but he could learn all he needed to know from me if he just asked. But then the man takes off his helmet and I know exactly *why* he hasn't bothered to ask me.

"Who is that?" I ask my sister pointing to the fireman who burnt our bookshop down.

She resolves her sniffling for a moment to answer my question. "Beckett Campbell." She says, confusion lacing her tone.

Campbell? Oh... no.

"Old high school friend of mine. He's the fire chief now. I'm surprised you don't recognize him from when we were younger. He happened to be driving by, he called the rest of the staff in when he saw the flames."

Of course he fucking did. So my suspicion was right, it was the arsonist who called in my rescue. I don't know if I should be grateful or annoyed.

He starts to approach the two of us and my stomach starts doing backflips over itself. I hadn't seen him in so long and he's gotten so much older, but I still can't believe I didn't recognize him. Trauma will do that to you. He crouches down next to me. "How are you doing?" His gruff cadence, warm with concern that I'm more than positive is fucking fake.

"Fine." I grit out.

"When I pulled you out of the flames I didn't think you were even breathing." He says softly. "I'm sure you don't remember much but, is there anything you can tell me?"

I stare at him in shock.

How the hell am I supposed to tell the fire chief about the man who started the fire when they are the same fucking person? I must have been quiet for longer than I thought because eventually he says, "*Do you* remember anything?" And stupidly I just shake my head.

"No." I whisper.

He smiles softly. "That's okay. We can try again later and see if maybe we can jog that memory at all."

"Beckett, I've gotta make a call. I just haven't wanted to leave her alone." Bridget says. "Can you stay with her?"

I swallow hard, but he nods. "Of course." The second Bridget is out of earshot he purrs, "That's a good girl."

I glare at him immediately and check behind me for the EMT, but they are over talking to another one of the firefighters. "I know what you did." I sneer.

"But you didn't say anything." He smirks.

"Not yet." I correct.

"You're not going to say anything, firebug." He growls. "Because if you do, it just so happens that Quinn O'Brady bought a bunch of lighter fluid and starter bricks off the internet and ordered them to the bookshop. And it just so happens the insurance payout on this place is partially in your name, as well as your sister's and your father's. So it wouldn't look so good on you if someone chose to chalk this up to anything other than an accident."

My eyes go wide. "You're framing me..." I whisper. It's not a question. "How did you know I would be here?"

Beckett shrugs. "I didn't. Just a coincidence."

"All this over what, an over a decade old grudge?" I shake my head. "I can't believe you're doing this to me."

He moves closer to me. "I'm not doing anything to you, firebug, because this was an accident," He leans back on his heels but stays crouched down. "Right?"

I nod, not knowing what else to do. "Right."

"Good girl." He purrs. "Now let's talk about that *anything* you promised me for saving your life."

I scoff at him. "You didn't save my life. You–"

"Called in the fire department and pulled you out of a burning building?" He hums.

I just blink at him. "You've got to be kidding me."

He nods. "I couldn't let you die." He purrs. "Not when you owe me such a big and such an open ended favor."

"I'm... I'm not giving you anything." I huff.

He pulls my oxygen mask off my face and my lungs immediately start trying to give up on me, hacking in ways that I've never experienced before. "I already set a building on fire, let's not assume murder is out of bounds for me either." He growls. "Your life is mine for the next two weeks. And then you can go back to your pretty little life in New York, your father can use the money from the insurance to rebuild, and I can finally get some sleep at night knowing those responsible got what they deserved."

I keep coughing until he puts the mask back over my face. "I hope you know there's a special place in hell-"

"For people like you?" He finishes. "Yeah, I could say the same thing, firebug." Beckett seems keen to continue torturing me but then he looks over his shoulder and sees Bridget approaching.

"I told dad you were okay," She says, "He's been worried sick about you, but I didn't tell him about the shop yet. I wanted one of us to be there in case he has a heart attack on the spot."

I just nod numbly, not really listening, distracted by the daggers that Beckett's hazel eyes are staring into my soul.

"I gotta go talk to him." Bridget finishes up, "I would ask you if you want to come with, but I think you should go to the hospital instead."

"I can go with her." Beckett purrs. "I'm off duty anyways."

"No!" I rush out and they both stare at me like I've lost my mind. "I just... I don't need to go to the hospital."

"Quinn," Bridget sighs. "You're being too stubborn. I just heard you hacking when I was on the phone with dad. Go to the hospital. I'll bring you a change of clothes once I calm dad back down and can get him in the car." She kisses me on the forehead and leaves, "Love you!"

Beckett smiles. "Guess that leaves you with me, firebug."

Fuck. I am so screwed.

Chapter Six

Quinn

"You have to testify." Beck pleads with me, his growing height taking up more of my room than I'm comfortable with. When my mother told me he wanted to come see me I didn't see the conversation going like this... I should have.

"I didn't see anything." I mutter out the lie, too young to truly understand the damage I was doing. Highschoolers don't consider just how real something like this is, I know I didn't.

He shakes his head. "That's a lie, Quinn and you know it!" He's right, but I don't like him saying as much so loudly.

I shush him, trying not to have my parents hear him from across the hall. I don't want *anyone to know about this. No one else needs to be exposed to the horrors I saw. Was that just the lie I told myself at the time to make this all better? Was that something someone fed to me and I just don't remember? "You're being too loud."*

"I'll be as loud as I fucking have to be." He growls. I cringe back at the word fucking, my sixteen year old self thinking it too taboo to be used so freely. "You need to testify, Quinn."

"I can't." I whisper. "You don't understand..."

"I don't understand!?" He roars. "You're helping cover up my sister's murder. What is there to not understand, Quinn? You're covering for Josh Ericson? Of all fucking people?"

"I'm not... You don't... You don't understand." I tell him again. "I can't." I stress the words hoping he will get what I'm trying to say to him, but I don't know if he's too clouded by rage.

He tilts his head at me, seeming to take my words in more carefully. "Someone is silencing you..." Beck just about snarls. "Who is it?"

"I don't know what you're talking about." I say robotically, but my eyes plead with him to understand why I have to keep quiet.

His eyes fill with something akin to pity, but not the kind that's understanding, the kind that's judgemental and full of thoughts that I should be doing more, doing better. "Quinn, what are they holding over you?"

I shake my head. "I don't know anything."

Beck moves to sit down on my bed, "Quinn," He says softly, "That animal murdered my sister. If you don't testify he could do it again to someone else. I know he did it, you told me you saw it. I know you saw it. Please, you have to testify."

I shake my head. "It was dark." I parrot the words I was taught to say. "I didn't see anything."

Beck huffs a laugh and it's one full of anger and sorrow. "You're willing to lie to protect some jock asshole? You know if they do call you to testify and you say that on the stand that it's perjury, right?"

"It was dark." I repeat. "I didn't see anything." I mutter again.

"Lila would be ashamed of you." Beck growls and stomps out of the room without another word.

Chapter Seven

Quinn

I slept a large part of the next day. Mostly from the exhaustion of the adrenaline wearing off but also because I had been up half the night before. My family left me be, figuring I was recovering from the ordeal and gave me the space to do so.

Intermittently I hear chattering downstairs and feel the guilt shoot through me; I know I should go check in on them, but that subsided because of the stress of thinking about Beckett and what the hell he wants from me.

He made some fairly vague comments about how, *we'd be in touch* when I got to the emergency room last night, and then left without much else. Somehow that was worse than him just telling me what he wants. It's the holidays, isn't it some kind of cardinal sin or something to blackmail someone during the holidays? If it's not it absolutely fucking should be.

I know why he's pissed, but there is absolutely nothing I can do about it now. After his sister was killed, the trial happened against Josh Ericson and when I didn't testify and Lila's journal went missing the whole case fell apart. Josh is still living in town with a wife now and some kids from what I hear. It's ancient history, but apparently Beckett never moved on.

I reach for my phone and find myself looking for flights back to New York, maybe I can just run from all of this. Maybe I can just disappear and go back home and if I never come back to this town then it's like everything that happened here didn't really happen. But as I'm looking through flights a text comes through.

The number is listed as Unknown and on it is a receipt for exactly what Beckett used to start the fire and my name on the top of it. My heart drops for a second before the next message comes through and the anxiety turns to anger.

Unknown: *If you book a flight, I'm sending this to the police along with the version of my report that says the fire was the work of a skilled arsonist.*

I roll my eyes, because did he really just complement himself as a *skilled arsonist?* The fucking audacity is wild.

Regardless of how annoyed I am, I decided to close the browser looking for flights since apparently going home early isn't going to be an option. But that then poses the question of how the hell he knew I was looking at flights in the first place. He must have some kind of something on my phone that's allowing him to watch the screen... He's put way too much effort into all of this.

Beckett should have just gone to therapy like a normal person, learned to cope with his sister's death, and *NOT* set a building on fire in some convoluted scheme for revenge. This is absolutely insane.

A knock sounds on my door. "Quinn?" Bridget calls from the other side.

"Yeah." I call back. "Come in."

She opens the door. "How are you feeling?"

"I told you last night I was fine." I say as neutrally as possible.

Bridget sighs. "Well, if you're fine then can you please come down and spend some time with everyone?" She nods. "The twins have been asking about you all day and dad has been worried with you hiding up here all day."

I sit up on the bed, adjusting my laptop on my legs. "Give me a second and I'll be right down."

"Don't take too long." Bridget says as she heads back down the stairs, leaving the door slightly ajar so I'm forced to, at least if nothing else, get up and go close it. But Bridget is right, I should go see my family while I'm here.

I force myself out of bed and change out of the t-shirt and pajama pants I've been lounging in all day and into a pair of fleece leggings and a green sweater. I grab my phone before I head down the stairs, taking a deep breath trying to settle myself. I don't know if Beckett is going to text again but if he does, I want to be by my phone.

"The insurance should come through as soon as the fire department is done with their inspection." Adriane says, leaning against the counter.

Ashley is prepping what appears to be a breakfast casserole, likely for tomorrow morning. "I still can't believe that happened. I have no idea how the fire could have even started. It's not like you had candles or a fireplace or anything."

I come to sit down at the high backed wooden barstools at the kitchen counter, swallowing my desire to tell them exactly what fucking happened.

"Beckett said it was probably an electrical fire." Bridget says, her gaze flickering to me. "I'm just glad that Quinn is okay." Her voice lowers, "That was way too close for comfort."

"Believe me, I agree." I mutter.

"How are you feeling?" My dad asks.

I fight the urge to snap at him and tell him that I'm more than fine like I've been telling everyone else. But something about his concern makes me check that instinct. "Shaken up." I answer honestly, but shortly. I don't know how much I can say without starting into a rant about Beckett.

"I can imagine." Ashley nods, whisking some eggs in a bowl. "Thank god that Beckett was nearby and saw the fire."

Yeah... Thank god.

I fight the anger off my face, I'm supposed to be grateful, technically the asshole did save my life. But no one else knows his reasons are more selfish than anything fucking else. "I–"

My phone starts ringing.

I pick it up off the counter and glance at the words *Unknown Caller* drifting across the screen. "I have to get this. It's a work thing." I just about beeline for the front door before anyone has a chance to say anything else.

As I pick up the phone I say, "Hold on." Into it, not even bothering to grab my coat as I rush out onto the porch to take the call.

"You don't give me orders," Beckett growls through the phone, "I'm the one holding all the cards here."

I shiver on the front porch, luckily I'm wearing heavy socks otherwise my feet would be absolutely freezing. "What do you want?" I growl.

"For you to get in the truck." He replies and it's only then that I notice a black ford sitting at the end of the driveway.

"I don't have shoes." I tell him, about to head back inside to go get some, but he stops me.

"You don't need them. We're just going to talk." Beckett pushes open the car door from the driver's seat. "Get in."

"My family is gonna wonder where I am." I challenge.

Beckett's shrug is audible. "Then we'll talk fast. But the longer you wait the more likely they are to start asking questions." His voice drops to an annoyed growl. "Now get in." He hangs up the phone.

I pad through the snow, trying to follow the footsteps that are set in the driveway already, but they only go so far. The wind whips through my hair, the coldness going bone deep as the snow soaks through my socks. I follow the tire tracks as best as I can to get down to his trucks and trudge through the last few feet to climb into his cab.

"Good girl." He purrs. "So you do know how to follow directions. Now close the door."

I do and refrain from calling him every dirty name in the fucking book even though he more than fucking deserves it. As he starts to drive off I buckle my seatbelt, not sure it's going to matter depending on what his plans are for me. He already almost killed me once, I wouldn't be surprised if he tried to kill me again.

"Where are we going?"

"That's enough questions." Beckett says. "I have some of my own." His eyes are fixed on the road but there is something behind them that's darker.

I shake my head. "What... what kinds of questions?" I'm trying to focus, but quite honestly, even with how much I'm annoyed with him, I can't help but notice the way his navy Henley is clinging to his biceps.

The truck speeds through the snowy backroads, having a lot better traction than my dad's since it's newer. "Where is Lila's journal?"

"I don't have it." I say just a little too quickly before he even has a chance to finish the question.

Beckett huffs. "You've always been a liar, firebug." He starts to pull onto the highway and I know all too quickly exactly *where* he is taking me.

"Turn around." I rush out. "Take me back."

He shakes his head. "You need to see it."

"I don't need to see anything." I've seen too much already. "Take me back, Beck." I find myself falling into the old nickname, my voice becoming desperate and I'm half tempted to jump out of the car. I probably would if he wasn't going sixty something right now.

"You forgot what happened." Beckett pushes. "So then this place should mean nothing to you. Why are you so upset if nothing happened, bug?" His voice is softer than I'd like, an ominous edge skirting around the outside of his words, making my stomach start to loop in on itself.

"Take me back. I'm not fucking around. Take me back. Now" I fight tears, trying to calm myself, calm my breathing, but he just keeps driving.

He glances over at me. "And you think I am fucking around?" He asks. "You want to claim you forgot. You want to claim you don't know anything. Maybe someone should jog your memory."

I pull my legs into myself on the seat, "Why are you doing this to me?" I mutter senselessly as I start sobbing softly. "I wasn't the one who killed her!" I shriek. "Why am I the one you're torturing?"

"Because you let her murderer fucking walk." Beckett growls. "You let Josh get away with it."

"My testimony wouldn't have changed any-thing!" I argue.

He scoffs. "Does telling yourself that make it easier to sleep at night in your satin sheets in your perfect apartment with your perfect life? Did you just forget about Lila? Bury what you saw in the recesses of your mind and pretend it never happened?"

"Of course I didn't forget Lila!" I cry out. "She was my best friend! I live in fear every day that something will happen to Madison. But you don't get to judge me for choosing not to let that fear rule my life! I choose to move forward. I don't understand why your inability to do the same should be my problem."

His eyes light with fire. "Move forward? My sister was raped and murdered and you just want me to move forward?" He shakes his head. "No. Everyone will fucking pay for what happened to Lila. Starting with you."

He pulls the truck off the highway towards the old park that is vacated for the win-ter. During the fall people love to come walk through the trails and see the beautiful leaves, none the wiser that my childhood best friend lost her life here.

The car stops and I no longer want to get out of it now, but Beckett snatches my phone out of my hands and reaches across me to open the car door. "Run, firebug."

I shake my head. "Take me back." I plead.

He opens his glove compartment and pulls out a knife. "I said *run*." He unbuckles my belt. "Feel how Lila felt. Know what you could have tried to save her from. What you let someone get away with."

My eyes stare at the knife. "You... You've got to be kidding."

The knife finds its way to my thigh, running up the inside of my leggings. "Do you want to find out?" He challenges before pulling the knife away. "I'll give you a head start. If I don't find you in an hour, I'll take you back home... If I do..." He smirks and my stomach drops. "Run, bug."

And this time he says it, I do.

Chapter Eight

Quinn

I just about fall on my face as I launch myself out of the truck and away from the fucking psycho holding the knife. He's going to kill me. He's going to fucking kill me and I'm going to end up just like fucking Lila. No one to know what happened to my body, just poof. Gone.

Fuck.

Why me? Why the fuck can't he be targeting Josh? He was the one who fucking killed Lila. I didn't kill Lila, I just didn't say anything.

My cold feet hurtle through the snow making me very very much wish I would have ignored Beckett and grabbed the fucking boots when I had the chance... Or maybe just have not gotten in the truck at all. I shouldn't have gotten in the fucking truck.

I'm such an idiot. Never let them bring you to a second location and what did I do? I hopped right into the truck without a second thought. Did I even hesitate?

In my defense though, Beck is smoking hot and always has been. The kinda hot that makes you not think straight. The kinda hot that makes you set your better judgement aside and do whatever the fuck he says. The kinda hot that makes running through the woods with him chasing me more than just a little erotic.

I need to focus. This man is trying to kill me.

The wind chills me as I race down the path but I quickly realize my footsteps in the snow are leaving a trail for him that leads straight to me. I don't really have time to think of a better plan since I don't know how far behind me he is. I can't really go off the path without shoes so I just keep running through the paved trail and hoping for the best.

My footsteps eat the ground beneath me and my head is on a swivel, continuously checking behind me for Beck. Beckett. Fuck. I can't do that. I can't let myself remember him as the teenager who was always annoying Lila. As the brother of my best friend.

I need to remember him as my would be killer. The man who lit my parents' shop on fire. The man chasing me through the woods right now without an ounce of remorse.

As I round a bend I realize the trail is about to split, half the split leads back out of the forest to a different parking lot. The other is a longer trail that will eventually reconnect with this one.

I freeze considering my options. If I go back on the other trail towards the parking lot I can try and reach the road from there in the hopes that someone will find me and save me.

If I run deeper into the forest I could hope that Beckett doesn't catch me and will keep his word about letting me go home in an hour. If I went towards the other parking lot some-one would want to know why I was running through the woods barefoot with no coat and I have no explanation for that. At least not one that won't piss off Beckett and I can't have him framing me for the fire.

So even if it probably is the stupider option, I make a few foot prints going off towards the parking lot before back tracking and running into the forest, but not on the trail, I go in between the trees.

I'm hoping he'll follow the more obvious set of foot prints rather than the ones I'm making now, but I'll have no way of knowing until it's too late. How am I supposed to know when an hour has passed without my phone anyways? I guess I won't know. I'll just have to keep running and do my best to guess.

It feels like at least twenty minutes have passed but that might just be the adrenaline. It's probably just the adrenaline. For all I know it could have only been a minute or two.

No... No it takes at least ten minutes to get to where the paths cross, even at an all out sprint. I used to run on these trails with Lila before everything happened. We used to practice for track and run on the trails two or three times a week.

So if I use that as a metric I've got another fifty minutes of running ahead of me... I'm way too out of shape for this. I work out, but only once a week at this point and I stopped doing heavy cardio years ago. This kind of stamina test is not something I'm prepared for.

I start to slow, but I don't stop because stopping could mean a knife in my back and I'm not willing to risk that. I could try counting and seeing if I can keep track of time that way, but that seems crazy. I–

I hear a whistle coming from behind me... too close behind me.

"Oh, firebug." Beckett sing songs into the trees. "That was a cute little diversion with the foot prints." He calls.

I need to start running again but my breathing is already ragged. I'm already exhausted. I know it hasn't been an hour, but I don't have adrenaline on my side anymore, all of it having been spent to get me as far as I have now.

"Shit. Shit. Shit." I mutter softly, not really even meaning too but the fear coursing through me is making it hard to think straight.

I look over my shoulder, expecting him to be somewhere in the treeline behind me, but he isn't... where did he–

My question is answered before I can even finish it as I feel him grab me around my waist. I shriek, my life flashing before my eyes and I'm sure he's about to fucking kill me. I go completely still when I feel the blade come to rest at my throat.

"It's not been an hour, firebug." He purrs into my ear, his knife starting to slide down my body without digging into my skin.

"I..." I fumble for my words trying to figure out if I should be begging for my life or for something else. Why do I want something else right now? My brain is fucking confused as hell and I should be terrified, but I'm not, I'm turned on. My body pushes into his in a way that it absolutely shouldn't be but instinct is a funny thing.

Beckett chuckles, the knife coming to slide under my sweater. "What was that?"

I shake my head. "Nothing." I rush out.

"Really?" He challenges. "Cause it feels like you just tried to fucking lean into me. While I'm holding a damned knife to your chest." He scrapes it against my skin in a way that I feel but doesn't draw blood. "Are you turned on right now?"

"No." I scoff.

"Liar." He pulls the knife away from my body and spins me around to pin my chest against a tree with him behind me. "Why do you always lie, Quinn? Maybe if you told the truth for a change, you'd actually get what you want."

I grit my teeth. "What I want is for you to get off of me and take me home."

"Is that really what you want, firebug?" He purrs in my ear.

"No." The word comes out too fast and without my brain even being able to think enough to stop it. Something about his words and the rumble in his tone spoke to my more primal instincts before the more logical part of me could assert its way to the forefront.

"What do you want, Quinn?" He purrs again in that same gruff cadence that makes my mind want to melt in the palm of his hands.

"You." I find myself admitting on an ex-hale.

He chuckles softly. "Was that so hard?" The smile in his voice audible as I hear the knife being tossed down into the snow beside us. He spins me around again but this time so my back is against the tree instead of my front. Beck presses his lips into mine and the second he does I'm reaching up to grab his shirt and ball it in my fists.

Beck pulls away again. "Telling the truth feels good, doesn't it, Quinn?"

I nod. "Yes." I whisper out as I pull him back closer to me and press my lips back to his. Our tongues swirl around each other in desperate strokes. I moan into the kiss and I want to take his shirt off but I'm worried about the cold.

Beck doesn't seem to share the same concerns because he's reaching down to the hem of my sweater and starting to pull it up and over my head. I let him blindly, and am immediately met with the chill of the wind. I shiver, feeling bare having forgot to put on a bra.

"This is a view I've been wanting to see for decades." Beck muses, his thumb running over my stomach. "I've had a fucking crush on you since middle school."

I shake my head. "You have a real funny way of showing it."

He nods. "I'm still pissed at you." He clarifies.

"Ditto." But contrary to my words my hands go to the bottom of his shirt and start to pull it up over his head. He lets me and we both toss the shirts down into the snow beside the knife.

Beck yanks down my leggings so they are around my knees and unzips his jeans. "Then we can agree that this is probably a mistake." He says as he pulls his cock out and pumps it a few times with his fist.

"Oh, absolutely a mistake." I nod, but he's lifting me up around my waist and helping seat me down onto his cock, using the tree for balance. "But I like making mistakes."

He scoffs as he thrusts into me. "I know you do, firebug."

I fight down the urge to argue with him as he starts to fuck me up against the tree. Our moans consume the air around us, our pleasure physically visible as the haze of frost is breathed out of our mouths and in each other's faces.

Beck's strokes are hard and unforgiving like he is more focused on himself than me and for some reason that's just making this fucking hotter. "What else do you want, Quinn?" He purrs into my ear, his body so close to mine that we are basically one fucking person in this moment.

"Your hand... Your hand around my throat." I admit.

Beck smiles and he doesn't hesitate. "Are you a little freak?" He groans again as his hand wraps around my neck and tightens with his stroke. "Do you like being tossed around and fucked like a slut, Quinn?"

I should tell him no, I should tell him to let me down, but I don't. "Yes." I moan, my better judgement apparently lapsing, frozen from the cold and unable to answer right now so I'm left with nothing but instinct and desire. "Yes, Beck." I moan again.

He groans. "I can't tell you how many times I dreamed of hearing you moan my name."

"Beck." I repeat and he groans again.

"That's a good girl." He says, thrusting into me.

The tree is abrasive on my back, scratching me all to hell and I feel the sensation so fully with the cold freezing me. I have a feeling my back is going to be bleeding from the bark digging into my skin, but that somehow is just turning me on more.

My nipples are stiff peaks even with Beck's body pressed against mine. I can feel my lips chattering and I'm sure they are blue now just like my toes. If I live past us finishing I'll be damned lucky if I don't end up with frostbite.

"Please." I beg softly. "Please don't kill me." I bounce myself as much as I can, using the tree for a backboard. My lips lock back on his. "Please." I moan between kisses trying to appeal to the side of him that decided to put his dick between my legs rather than the side that chased me through the woods.

Beck shakes his head. "I was never going to kill you." He promises as his hand snakes between the two of us and starts to rub roughly at my clit. "I couldn't even if I wanted to, Quinn. I don't think I would ever forgive myself if I was the reason something happened to you."

I find myself moaning again and this time not because of what he's doing between my legs even though that feels so fucking good. "You're insane." I mutter between gasps.

He just nods. "Yet you kissed me in a burning building." He says as his thumb kneads harder at my center, it hurts, but in that way that makes you want more. "Yet you jumped into my truck with no idea what I was going to do to you. Yet you're letting me fuck you." He gives a hard thrust. "If I'm insane, Quinn, what are you?"

I shake my head. "Just shut up and fuck me."

He lets go of my throat and I whimper. "You give orders, you don't get what you want." He growls. He's about to pull out of me when I dig my wet heels into his back.

"Please!" I cry. "Please fuck me, please."

Beck pauses. "Are you demanding or begging?"

"Begging." I rush out. "I'm begging. Please please fuck me, *Beck*."

He groans and he still hasn't pulled out yet, that gives me hope. "Apologize."

I bristle. "For what?" I huff.

"For lying about wanting me." He smirks, giving one hard stroke. "Apologize and I'll keep going." His promise is dark and sensual. While I don't want to apologize to him, I want to finish on his cock more.

"I'm sorry." I grit out.

"For?" He alludes.

"For lying." I grumble.

Beck smiles. "That's a good girl." He resumes his strokes and this time they are deeper. This time his hand moves between my legs with more skill and less desperation, like he's trying to lure me over the edge and it's fucking working.

"I want you to come for me, Quinn." He demands. "I've waited years to have your body writhing up and down on my cock. I'm done waiting. I want to feel you finish on my dick."

I nod feverishly and focus on what he's doing between my legs. It takes less than a minute for him to coax my body over the edge and then I'm screaming out my orgasm into his shoulder.

He follows me over the edge a second later finishing between my legs in a deep groan and a growl that has my mind melting into his hand. Beck lowers me back down to the ground and grabs my snow covered soaked sweater along with his shirt and hands mine back to me. "Get back to the truck, I need to take you home."

Chapter Nine

Quinn

When we get back to the truck and I start to warm up my hands and feet by the vents, I realize I did not in fact end up with frostbite. Beckett hands me back my phone and there are no less than twenty calls from my sister and about two hundred texts, I don't even know how she sent that many that quickly.

> *Bridget: Where are you?*
> *Bridget: What is going on?*
> *Bridget: Do I need to call the police?*
> *Bridget: Did you get eaten by a bear?*
> *Bridget: CALL ME!!!*

"She's been blowing up your phone since shortly after you ran from the truck." Beckett says.

I sigh, my head kicking back in frustration before I right myself again so I can put my hands and feet back by the vents. "What do you want me to tell her?"

He shrugs. "You can tell her that you're with me. We learned our lesson about lying, didn't we Quinn?" He purrs, his hand slipping between my legs to massage my pussy.

I nod feverishly even though what I want to be doing is rolling my eyes. This man already has me all kinds of fucked up. "I should call her." I tell him, waiting for him to pull his hand out from between my legs, but he doesn't.

"Then call her." But his hand slips into my leggings and finds my clit easily with the car still parked.

"How am I supposed to call her when you're doing that?" I grumble, only slightly annoyed.

Beck shrugs. "I'm sure you'll figure it out."

I huff. "Maybe I'll just text her." But then he's grabbing the phone out of my hand with his free one and pressing the call button. I glare at him and when I do he rolls his thumb over my clit, deliberately trying to fuck with me. This phone call is going to be painful.

"Hello." Bridget rushes out. "Quinn is that you?"

"Yes." I tell her. "It's me. I'm fine, Bridge."

"Where are you?!" She shrieks into the phone. "You said you had a work call and I went to check on you after like fifteen minutes and you were GONE! What the hell, Quinn?"

"Bridge, calm down." I tell her but my voice is hitching because Beck is pinching my clit between his fingers rather roughly. "I'm with Beck. He came by to check on me and we wanted to catch up so we went for a drive."

"Without your shoes?" Bridget huffs. "Or your coat? Or your purse? You just hopped into his truck and abandoned everything?"

I don't really have any answer to that.

"You haven't called him Beck in *years*." She says, her tone full of correct accusations. "You expect me to believe that you just jumped in Beckett Campbell's truck to *talk*?"

"Bridge." I whine softly into the phone.

Beckett finds that moment to slip his fingers inside of me, the jackass, and curls them in a come hither motion that has me fighting a moan.

"If he's there then put him on the phone." Bridget says, seeming sure she caught me in some kind of lie.

"Hi, Bridget." Beckett says, taking the phone from me. He takes it off speaker and puts it up to his ear. "Yeah, she's fine." A pause. "Yes, we did." Another pause. "Not originally but I was optimistic." He chuckles. "I'll have her home in a half hour." He hangs up and hands the phone back to me. "There."

"Did you just tell her that we hooked up?" I stare at him dumbfounded.

Beckett chuckles. "She asked." He shrugs.

My mouth is agape but he quickly turns that into gasps as he continues to work my pussy with his hand. "You know honesty doesn't mean you need to tell everyone everything?" I grumble. "You could have just said that it was none of her business."

"Why?" Beck purrs, leaning into me, "Are you ashamed of hooking up with me, Quinn?"

"No." I lie.

He pulls his hand away. "If you had been honest and just said yes. I would have let you finish on my fingers."

I grumble as I watch this man start to lick his fingers clean, slowly, clearly just trying to

fucking torture me further. The aching between my legs is making me want to fucking
scream. But then a thought hits me. "Are you
okay?"

He looks at me a little confused. "Yeah,
why?"

"I mean... you did just fuck me in the same
forest your sister died in." I say more seriously
now. "If that's not a fucking cry for help, I don't
know what is."

"So the arson didn't count as a cry for help?"
Beck chuckles like it's a joke but my face stays
serious. He sighs when he looks over at me,
putting the truck in reverse and start to back
out of the parking spot. "I've been struggling
for a long time, but *that?*" He nods to the
forest. "That was oddly therapeutic. More
so than any of the actual therapy my mother
made me go to."

Now I'm even more fucking confused. "How
so?"

He shrugs. "Cause I rewrote history." He
puts the car in drive and starts to pull out
onto the road. "You actually wanted me. I
didn't kill you. Both of us walked out alive.
And what happened to my sister didn't happen

again because I was in control this time, not some asshole with no morals."

I just kinda blink at him for a second, trying to put his fucked up logic together in my brain.

"I mean, did that not help you to feel some sort of... I don't know closure?" He asks.

I shake my head. "I hadn't thought about it."

The two of us are quiet for most of the drive back as I try to process what the fuck he just said. In a way he's right, it did kind of help because it replaced a bad memory with a good one. That place won't be where my best friend died when I think back on it, it will be where I got my brains fucked out of me by one of the hottest men I've ever met.

Madison has some kind of sixth fucking sense so it's in that moment that my phone goes off and of course it's her.

Mads: How's your day been?

Now given she may have just completely texted me by coincidence, but I'm just saying the timing is beyond fucking convenient.

Me: You were right, I should have brought condoms.

I follow it up with a winky face, an eggplant emoji, and the three water droplets.

Madison sends back the skull and cross bones emoji.

Mads: *I'm always right, thank you very much. How was he? WHO was he?*

"Who is that?" Beckett asks, nodding at my phone.

I text Madison back first.

Me: *I'll call you later.*

I add an eyes closed, tongue out emoji before I turn my phone off and focus my attention back on Beckett. "Why?" I ask. "Are you jealous?"

He kinda glances over at me for a second before returning his gaze back to the road in front of him. Another stretch of silence passes between us before he finally says, "I want Lila's journal."

I shake my head softly. "I don't have it." And technically that's not a lie. I don't have it, but I do know where it is.

"You do." He corrects. "I spent a lot of time trying to figure out what happened back then and the last person I was able to track the journal to was you, Quinn."

"I don't have it." I just repeat, being more careful with my words since he seems to have figured out some kind of tell to know when I lie. "I swear, I don't."

Beckett pauses for a second seeming to analyze what I said, like he's putting the pieces together. "But you know who does?"

"No one has it, Beckett." I tell him, my voice harsher as he pulls up next to my dad's house. "No one needs to have it either. It's better off if that journal says gone. Trust me on that."

He puts the car in park. "I'm going to find it, Quinn." And it feels like an ominous warning. "And you're going to help me."

I just shake my head again and hop out of the truck. "Some things are better off left in the past."

"I'm sorry, so you had a best friend before me!?!" Madison huffs through the phone.

"Mads, focus." I chide softly. "I can't let him get that journal." I tell her, pacing back and forth on the porch, this time with my shoes and coat. It was the only place I could get some privacy since my room isn't sound proof.

She sighs through the phone. "You know you probably shouldn't have told me any of this until you got back home right? This line could so easily be tapped" I know she is right because Beckett has already proved he's watching my phone so I'm sure he's heard this whole conversation, but the brief giggling and talk about sex I don't really care if he hears. I know better than to say where the journal is. Ever.

"He is if no one else." Which I really wish I had thought of when I called her, but I was too distracted... by a number of things if I'm being honest.

"Hi Beckett." Madison replies, her voice smiley but I know her well enough to know it's fake.

I hear a text ping. "Hold on."

Unknown: *Tell her I say hi back.*

"Can't you just text me from your actual number like a normal person?" I grumble into the phone. "Texting me from some random unknown number makes you look like a stalker."

Beckett: *Better?*

"Yes actually." I don't remember saving him as a contact, but he did have my phone for at least an hour earlier today.

"He's texting you, isn't he?" Madison asks.

I nod even though she can't see it. "Yeah. And he's being a real jackass." I hear my phone go off again but I don't check it this time. "But the journal?"

"Well he knows you know where it is. If for no other reason that you just admitted it." Madison replies. "Kinda dumb, Quinn. Did you just forget he was tapping your phone?" Yes, but I'm not about to say as much. "Personally I think you should just let him have it."

"I can't do that."

"I don't see why not. Lila is dead, he isn't and if he wants to torture himself with whatever's between those pages then why is it your responsibility to stop him?" She makes a good point even if I hate it, but no, I can't just give it to him.

"Lila asked me to hide it." I admit and the second the words leave my mouth another text chime sounds off. "She didn't want anyone to read it and I don't know what Beckett plans to do with the journal, but I want to honor what Lila wanted."

Madison sighs again, "And while that's honorable, Quinn, it sounds like you don't really have a choice. I think you should really consider what he can do with the leverage he has over you. You could end up in jail for gods know how long. Not to mention that your sister and your dad could be easily framed as accomplices."

"I... I don't think he'll actually do it." But as the words come out, I'm chewing on my lip. I don't know for sure though. Do I trust that his bigger priority is keeping everyone out of jail rather than this journal?

"Do you want to risk it?" She asks.

No.

My phone goes off again and this time I do check it.

Beckett: Call me a jackass again, see if I still give you a Christmas present.

Beckett: Where???

Beckett: You don't want to know how far I'll go, firebug. Give me the fucking journal.

I grumble and sigh, loud and exasperated and most of all exaggerated, specifically for Beckett's benefit. "I-" I don't know what I was going to say next but whatever it was is cut off by Bridget coming out onto the porch.

"Oh, so you are still here this time." Bridget leans against the doorframe.

I nod. "Yeah. I'm just on the phone."

"With Beckett?" She asks.

I stop my pacing, trying to calm myself and find a place to pause on the railing. "No, it's... it's Madison." My phone goes off again and I fight my urge to sneer at it.

Beckett: Well I guess that's technically true, but you are texting me.

"Is that Beckett?" She asks, hearing my phone go off in my hand.

"Quinn, I'm gonna let you go." Madison says through the speaker. "Call me later when you have a second and we can talk about that book." I know she's not talking about *her* book in this instance.

"I'll talk to you later, Mads." And then she hands up the phone. I have no idea if Beckett can still hear me now, but I tuck the phone in my pocket speaker side down in the hopes of muffling it if he can. "What's up?"

Bridget shrugs, "Just checking on you. You've been out here for over a half hour and last time you were, you disappeared having hopped in the truck of someone you haven't seen in over a decade."

I run a hand through my hair as I lean back onto the railing. "I'm fine, Bridge."

"Beckett is bad news, Quinn." Bridget says. "You shouldn't have gotten in that truck, let alone let him..." She steps outside and closes the door. "Well, you know."

"I'm fine, Bridge." I tell her again. "I'm an adult, I can take care of myself. I know you feel like you have to look out for me, but I'm fine."

Bridget wraps her arms around herself, having not grabbed a jacket and only having on her flannel. "Quinn, you're my little sister, I will always protect you. It's what older sisters do." She shivers a little. "And with everything that happened when we were teenagers... I'm just worried that Beckett is hanging around you for the wrong reasons."

I just nod, not being able to refute that since, he absolutely is around for the wrong reason, but I can't tell Bridget that. I don't think she'd understand why I hid the journal in the first place. "I'll be careful." I lie.

She just nods back. "Now come back inside and spend some time with your family while you're here."

Chapter Ten

Beckett

The house is cold as I walk inside. I haven't had the heart to sell it even though no one lives here now. My place is across town, as far away as I could get at the time.

The furniture sits exactly as it was, a gray blue sectional takes up most of the living room, but it's covered in dust now. Everything is covered in dust now. The old TV that my mother never replaced sits with its broken screen in the center of the wall. I remember my fist going through it the night my mother died.

She had struggled with cancer for years on and off, but this last time it finally took her. I think my father being gone was what made the difference. She didn't want to go on without him even if he was a deadbeat.

He was never a good parent growing up and when Lila passed, he only got worse. I don't know how someone as sweet as my mother could end up with someone as cruel as my father, but maybe it's that opposites attract thing. Maybe it's that she saw something in him that no one else did. But whatever she saw in him, he ran away with his mistress about six years ago and a year after that, my mom was gone.

I haven't heard from him since. He hasn't reached out to me and I didn't bother to reach out to him. I always tried to shield Lila from him, he could do what he wanted to me as long as he left Lila alone.

Maybe that's why she didn't recognize a toxic man when she saw one. She thought every man just acted like my father so when Josh treated her like my mother she thought that was normal.

I may not be able to sell this place... but I do have other plans for it.

I slowly start placing the fire starters and fireworks around the house, through the living room, kitchen and the office on the first floor. I climb the stairs and a slew of memories hit me full of Lila, full of my mother. The only two good people I've ever known in this world, both taken from me.

The people responsible get to go on living their lives like nothing ever happened. They get to run off to Vegas with a girl twenty years their junior. They get to go to college and get out of this town. They get to start a family. And where am I? Stuck in a house with nothing but ghosts to keep me company.

I pull the lighter fluid out of my bag and start dosing my childhood room. I don't want anything in here. I don't need any of it. All I need is that journal.

That journal can pinpoint Lila's killer. It says where she went and who she went there with the night of her death, I know it does. I got to see it before Quinn managed to sneak it out of evidence. I still don't know how she did that.

I walk over to Lila's room and I almost hesitate to start with my next bottle of lighter fluid. I almost think maybe some part of her soul is living in this room and I should leave her intact, but I can't.

No.

It's time for this place to go.

I start dosing her bed with the clear liquid making sure the mattress and bookshelf are soaked down since those things are the most flammable.

Once I spray down the rest of the rooms I put down all the other fireworks I light up a cigarette. Smoking is a nasty fucking habit, but I picked it up because I liked the excuse to watch the fire dance in the lighter before I actually lit it. I will never understand vaping.

I breathe the smoke into my lungs and ex-hale the release knowing this place will soon not be able to haunt me any longer. Once I've smoked about half of it I toss it onto my bed and wait a second before I leave to make sure the mattress actually goes up. It does and when it does I smile watching the small flame grow and spread.

I head down stairs and stop in the kitchen, my eyes drifting to the china cabinet. Hell, this night is about stress relief. Walking over to the cabinets I think about how angry my mother got the one time I broke one of her plates.

Sorry mom.

I pick up the first plate, raise it high above my head and toss it hard down to the ground with a resounding shatter. The crack rings through the house and it's at that time I start hearing one of the fireworks shooting off that was left upstairs, probably the one in my bedroom. I take the next plate and break that one and the next and the next until they are all broken and shattered around the room.

My eyes catch on the liquor cabinet and immediately realize that might help with the fire. I start tossing liquor bottles down throughout the house, any that are plastic I just pour out onto the rugs and then throw behind me. The place reeks of alcohol and that being reminiscent of my childhood only furthers my conviction to see this place burn.

I light another cigarette downstairs and lean against the front door as I watch the place go up in flames around me. Once the cigarette is just about finished I toss it into the flames.

"Good riddance." I walk out the front door, and I never look back.

Chapter Eleven

Quinn

Lila pushes some of her dark brown hair out of her face before playing with the ends of the strands. "I think I'm going to go see him tonight." She scribbles something into her journal but I don't see what it is at the time.

I sit back against her headboard. "Lila, are you sure that's a good idea? What if he wants more than just a kiss?" I don't trust her boyfriend, Josh, as far as I can throw him, and I'm not particularly strong.

She waves me off. "He cares about me." She says naively, "He said as much and I trust him not to hurt me."

I should have fought her harder on that. I should have told her that he was a douche and that he absolutely would hurt her. Even back then him being a psychopath was apparent, I just was too young to know I should be doing something about it.

Lila closes her journal and pushes up from her chair, reshelving the journal on her small book shelf over the desk. "You're too much of a worrier, Quinn." *She comes to sit back down on the bed.* "You always think everything is going to go wrong."

Yes, and I'm usually right, not that I told you so does absolutely anything for anyone now. "I just don't want you to be disappointed, Lila. I just don't want you to find out he isn't the guy you think he is."

"He is the guy I think he is, Quinn." *She insists.* "He's sweet to me. He gave me his pencil in homeroom when I told him I forgot mine." *She leans in.* "And can I tell you a secret?"

I nod.

"I actually did have a pencil." *She whispers like it's the most scandalous thing either of us could dream of at that point in our lives.*

I chuckle at her joke and lean in too, "Very cunning."

Lila bobs her head excitedly. "Yeah, I just can't believe he actually asked me out. And our first date was so nice, it makes going some-where private less scary because I trust him not to go too far."

I just nod again.

She glances at the clock on her desk. "I need to go." She straightens her shirt a little and goes over to her window. "If anyone knocks just tell them I'm asleep. They shouldn't come in without asking."

"Are you sure about this?" I ask again.

Lila just waves me off. "I'll be fine." And then she climbs out the window without an-other word. I watch her as she slides down the roof like she has countless times when she sneaks out and runs down the street to Josh's truck.

The sinking feeling in my stomach doesn't go away as I start reading one of the books our English teacher assigned us for the semester. I try to focus on the book, I try not to worry about Lila. She should be back in a couple hours and then we can go to bed and Beck will drop us off at school in the morning.

Everything is fine.

A knock sounds at the door.

I rush to answer it before whoever is on the other side can open the door and see Lila is gone. I peek my head out and see Beck standing there holding some bedding.

"I just wanted to make sure you had something to sleep on. Lila's trundle is usually bare so I brought you a blanket and pillow." He says passing the items to me.

"Thanks." I take them with a soft smile and try to keep an eye on how wide I open the door. Her bed isn't visible from it, but better safe than sorry.

"How have you been?" He asks. "I've been so busy with work I feel like I haven't seen you around in a while."

"Good." I say peeking back over my shoulder, checking the window since Lila could be back any minute. It's been about an hour.

Beck tilts his head looking at me confused. "Is something wrong, Quinn?"

"No." I rush out. "No, it's fine. Lila is just changing." The lie comes out smoothly but something in Beck's eyes makes me feel like he caught it even before he's pushing open the door to the bedroom.

"What's going on, Quinn?" As the door opens he looks around and immediately notices a distinct lack of a changing Lila. "Where did Lila go this time?" He sighs.

I shake my head. "I..."

Beck grabs me by the arm and starts dragging me in my pajamas out of the room and down the hallway towards the front door. "Let's go."

I slip on my shoes that are by the front door and follow Beck to his truck. It's an older one that was a hand me down from his uncle, but the fact that he has a car at all is lucky. I climb into the cab on the passenger side and he turns the engine over.

"Where did she go?" Beck asks as he pulls back down the driveway, stopping before he gets onto the main road.

"Can't we just go back inside, she will be home soon."

"Where did she go?" Beck asks again, his tone leaving little room for argument.

My hands play in my lap. "The trails." I whisper softly.

"Why?" He pulls the car out onto the road and takes off much faster than I would like towards where Lila is.

"She's meeting Josh." My hands are cold in the truck, the chill in the air not quite gone yet as spring is starting to take hold.

I don't remember much else from the rest of that night. I suppressed a lot of it when I left home, on purpose or just because it was easier I don't know. But I do remember bits of Lila in the woods, blood, and running back towards Beck before Josh saw me.

Beck saw how shaken up I was and asked me what happened, then he went charging into the woods and found Lila, but not Josh. The last thing I actively do remember from that night is sitting in a police station until three in the morning with my parents holding me and my best friend gone.

Chapter Twelve

Quinn

Beckett was quiet most of the next day and honestly that felt more ominous than if he would have been blowing up my phone bugging me for the journal. I have half a mind to text him and ask him what the fuck he's planning but I sincerely doubt he'd actually tell me.

I watch the slats in the ceiling from the guest bed, like they will somehow have the answers to all of my problems. Like the tones in the wood will magically take me back home and make everything alright. Unlikely. Maybe I shouldn't have stopped believing in Santa so young, I sure could use some Christmas magic right about now.

Bridget and Adriane have already gone home and shortly after they left I went to go hide in the guest room. I've been texting Madison for the past hour trying to convince her to send me that manuscript and she's been fucking teasing me about it.

Me: Mads, come on please.

Madison: Is there the one that's possessive or is it they're? I can never remember.

She follows it up with a thinking emoji and I want to fucking scream. I know that she's not making stupid mistakes like that but at the same time, I want to check for myself because if there is a *their* spelled like *there* I want to be the one to fucking tell her as much.

Me: MADISON

Madison: Should I be spelling it differently? Like theire for all of them?

And then she punctuates that with a smiling halo emoji.

Me: PLEASE JUST SEND IT TO ME

Madison: Okay, fine! I've fucked with you long enough. I'm sharing it with you now.

Excitedly I pull out my laptop and check my email for her, refreshing it constantly and thanking god that she finally relented. I get the notification but then I start to hear something down the hallway.

My door is cracked open a little, but I can't make out what exactly the sound is. I set my laptop back down and start to make my way towards the hall. The sound gets louder and I hear it coming from downstairs. It almost... It almost sounds like crying.

I pad my way across the hall on silent feet, trying not to alert my dad to my presence and as I get closer to the staircase the crying becomes more notable. I've never heard my dad cry before. There's a sniffle and a sigh, some breaths trying to calm the tears followed by the sobbing continuing on anyways.

I don't... I don't know how to handle this situation. Does he want me to go talk to him? Do I just leave it alone and pretend I didn't hear anything?

The selfish part of me wants to go for the latter. I want to just go back into my room, close the door, and read what Madison sent me. It should be really fucking good too. She was talking about how it's some kind of vacation romance centered around a billion-aire/assistant trope.

But... that's wrong, isn't it? I shouldn't just leave him to his own devices. I've spent too long letting my sister be the one to take care of my dad and he's my parent too.

If it was my mom I wouldn't hesitate. I would go right down the stairs and ask her what is wrong. I would go make her a cup of tea and talk to her until she felt better.

"Dad?" I call as I climb down the stairs towards the kitchen.

He is sitting in one of the chairs at the island with his head in his hands. "Quinn." He sobs softly, clearly trying to get it together and failing.

I walk over to the kettle and pick it up off the counter, going to the sink to fill it with water. "What's going on?" I ask, as I set it down on the base and turn it on.

He just kind of shakes his head. "I'm fine."

I move to the cabinet and grab out a couple mugs. "Is chamomile okay?" He nods as I move over to grab the tea bags. Once I put the bags in the cups, I stand across from him on the center island and wait quietly for him to speak again.

He doesn't.

The dark kitchen is silent except for the sounds of the kettle warming. Wind rustles up against the windows as snow comes down outside and I want to go rest a hand on the cold glass. The water comes to a boil and I pour it into both the cups, passing him one.

"Thank you, Quinn." His tears have slowed as he stares down at the cup.

"What's going on?" I ask again, adding some sugar to my cup before passing the shaker that was on the counter to him.

He takes it and adds some to his cup as well before putting it back in the center of the island next to the salt and pepper. "I'm fine." But his voice cracks as he says it.

"Is it about mom?" I try and when he looks away from me I feel like I hit a nerve. I don't know what to do so I just grab spoons out of one of the drawers and hand him one before stirring my tea with the other.

He doesn't say anything for a long while, he doesn't stir his tea, he just looks into the hot beverage, steam rolling off the top of it and runs his fingers over the handle.

When I think the tea has become cool enough to drink, I take a sip and I'm thankful that it didn't burn my tongue. The soft floral taste is comforting and I let myself get absorbed in the warmth.

"Your mother loved that bookshop."

I look up at him. "Yeah, she did."

"She loved the holidays too." He drinks a little of his own tea then. "She would have been trying to make the best of this situation. Jenna would have been talking about how this could be a fresh start for the new year and maybe we could attract new business by having a grand reopening." He chuckles, but the sound is empty and tired. "But all I see is that what my wife and I spent our lives building is gone."

I nod softly. "I'm sorry." It's not my fault, not really, but it feels like it is. It feels like if I had just testified all those years ago that none of this would have happened. Josh would have gone to jail, Beckett wouldn't have spent years holding his grudge, The Maple Corner Bookshop would still be standing and not a pile of ash blowing away in the winter wind.

He shakes his head. "It's not your fault, Quinn" And some part of me needed to hear him say that. Something in me believes him more than myself. "I thank god that Beckett found the store burning and got you help. I don't... If I would have lost you too... The store, that's replaceable, you're not."

I nod again not really knowing how to respond to that. We drink the rest of our cups of tea in silence and eventually we are both done, I take the cups and set them in the sink to be cleaned tomorrow. "You'll get the bookstore back." I promise him.

"I hope so, Quinn." He smiles softly as he pushes up off the counter and heads upstairs.

I pull my phone out of my pocket and look for the text chain with Beckett. He has to file the report that it's an accident, that's the only way my dad can rebuild and I won't let him lose the bookshop for good, not after he's already lost my mom. This is about him and I owe it to him.

I'm sorry, Lila.

Me: I'll show you where the journal is. Come by the house tomorrow night around six.

The response back is immediate.

Beckett: I'll be there, firebug.

Chapter Thirteen

Quinn

"No babe, we are not getting a pet duck, we already have a baby on the way." Adriane sighs, leaning back into Bridget on the couch.

Bridget rubs gently at Adriane's bump as they cuddle, "I'm not saying we get a duck right this second, I'm just saying that we *could* get a duck. Maybe in a year or two."

Adriane laughs. "Still no, babe."

I fight the urge to call her a buzzkill even if I don't necessarily agree with my sister's idea. They absolutely don't need a duck.

I'm reading through chapter two of Madison's book, but I've had to read this page no less than ten times because I get about half way through it before Bridget calls my attention again. At least I had some time this morning to get some work done.

"Addie." Bridget whines. "Ducks are cute and I would take care of them."

"Oh so now it's them?" Adriane laughs. "What happened to 'just one please just one?' Now we are getting multiple ducks?"

Bridget's fingers run through Adriane's hair. "Well you can't just get one duck. They would get depressed. Ducks are social creatures! They need friends."

"You said the same thing after we got the first cat and now we have three and none of them get along." Adriane chuckles.

Bridget waves her off. "That's just because-" She's cut off as the doorbell rings. "Who is that?" Bridget moves to stand but stops when she sees me set down my laptop.

"Beckett." I answer.

"Why?" Bridget's brow furrows in clear frustration.

"Because I invited him over." I say simply, pushing off the other couch and going to get the door. I take a quick breath before I answer it, forcing myself to stabilize. He doesn't need to see the anxiety I feel right now, I'd prefer if no one saw it honestly.

"Are you okay?" Bridget eyes me in that way big sisters do when they are sure something is wrong and they are trying to determine just exactly what it is.

I shake the lead out and open the door. "Hi."

"Hello, Quinn." Beckett purrs and my stomach drops. His hazel eyes scan me and he also seems to recognize the nerves coursing through me. Beckett leans in. "How's your Christmas Eve Eve?"

"Eventful." I clip out.

He chuckles and leans back. "Are you going to invite me in, or would you rather we just sit in the doorway all night?"

I honestly consider that for a second. "I'll meet you outside in a minute." I tell him and just about shove Beckett back out the door before slamming it in his face. There is a distinct grumble as he stumbles backwards, having apparently been caught off guard by the shove.

"Why is he here?" Bridget asks again.

I grab my jacket off the coat rack next to the door and start to shoulder it on. "Don't worry about it." Slipping my shoes on, I just about run out the door before my sister has a chance to ask any more questions.

"I'm going to make you pay for that." Beckett says the second the door closes.

I just walk past him and start heading towards the back of the house. I don't really want to know just *how* he intends to make me pay for that because I have a distinct feeling his idea is something vaguely sexual and while that does sound somewhat appealing, I'd rather just get him the journal and get him out of my life. Sex with him was a mistake, one that doesn't need to happen again.

"Taking me out back to shoot me, Quinn?" Beckett asks on a chuckle.

I glare at him as I twist the numbers to the padlock on the shed. "That's not funny." I pull the lock off and put it in my pocket before yanking the shed doors open.

"I thought it was funny." He says. "Well as long as you don't actually plan on doing it." When I level a stare at him, I'm surprised to see him look a little scared.

"No." I respond before pulling two shovels off the wall of tools. I shove one into his hand and head back out of the shed, locking it behind me. "But that doesn't mean I haven't considered it." I mutter.

Beckett chuckles but the sound is hollow. "This to bury my body then?" He asks. "Gonna make me dig my own grave?"

I shrug. "Maybe."

"Kinky." He says and I glare at him again as I start heading into the woods behind my parents' property. He follows me for a second before grabbing my arm and pulling me to a stop. "Are you actually going to try and-"

"No, paranoid." I grumble. "I buried the journal. That's where I'm taking you." And apparently however he knows when I lie didn't flag for him because he believes me.

We walk for a few minutes, my eyes scanning the trees trying to find the marking I made to know where the box was. I put it pretty low but it had to have grown by now, I just have no idea by how much. It takes about ten minutes of walking around in circles, all of which Beckett spent bitching about how long we had been walking, before I finally spotted the mark and stopped.

"Here." I tell him and walk between the spaces in the trees. "It should be right about here, just maybe like two or three feet down."

Beckett doesn't hesitate. He digs his shovel into the snowy ground right where I said it would be and doesn't even seem to mind when I just move out of his way. His determination is something scary.

His hands strain in his gloves from how tight he is gripping the shovel's handle. He furrows his brow more and more the deeper he digs like he's starting to get frustrated. "If it's not here." He grumbles after a few minutes.

"It is." I tell him, not bothering to help now since he must be nearly to the lock box. I lean against my shovel, using it for balance to keep upright in my boredom. I don't love that he's getting the journal, but I've made peace with that this is what has to happen.

"Quinn." He growls, digging deeper and right as I'm sure he's about to start cursing me out, there's a clank against his shovel. The anger in his face dissipates and he tosses the shovel to the side and just about dives to the ground to pull out the lock box.

"What's the code?" He growls.

I walk up to him, take the box, and twist the numbers. "Lila's birthday." I whisper softly and the box clicks open.

Beckett yanks it out of my hands and I don't try to stop him or object. This is something he's apparently spent years looking for, I can understand why he's blinded by the need to see it. He opens the box and just kind of stares at it for a second.

"You're fucking with me." He growls and throws the box to the ground. It's only in that moment that I realize the box is empty. The weight should have been a tip off but I didn't notice.

I start backing up as he advances on me, prowling forwards with eyes full of fury. "Beckett. I hid it here." I tell him, grabbing a hold of my shovel, using it to try and put some space between the two of us.

He seems to hesitate for a second, but then he grabs the shovel by the blade and yanks it roughly out of my hand. I gasp as he throws it to the side and it slams against a tree. "WHERE IS THE JOURNAL?!" He roars.

"I... I don't know." I stare down at the box confused. "This is where I put it. I left it here." I swear. "I don't... I don't know what happened to it if it's not here."

He shakes his head. "You're lying. You always lie." He growls, still advancing on me and backing me into a tree. "You just found some way to subvert your tell." He cages me in, placing his arms on both sides of me on the tree.

"I'm not, I swear." Fear races through me and not in that same way it did last time we were alone in the woods together, this fear is real. The kind that makes you want to break down and fall to pieces. Tears prick at my eyes that I try to fight because I don't want him to see just how terrified I am of him in this moment. "I don't know where it is if it's not here." I assert, but my voice cracks.

Beckett watches me with hard eyes and as the tears start to spill over he just about stumbles backwards. "You... you actually don't know... and that makes me a gigantic fucking dickhead." He takes another step away from me. "I'm... I'm sorry, Quinn."

I just storm past him, no longer caring about the shovel or the hole in the ground that someone needs to fix or anything fucking else instead of getting as far away from this man as possible. Bridget was right, I should have listened to her and just stayed away from him. I should have just ran the risk of him framing me and figured something else out. I make plenty of money, I could have started a Go-

FundMe or something to rebuild the book-store. I didn't have to sell my soul.

"Quinn, wait!" He calls from behind me.

"Leave me alone, Beckett." I try to keep my tone as level as possible as I continue to *run* from the man. The snow coming down between the trees is starting to get in my hair as I flee and the tears in my eyes are quickly getting uncomfortable as they freeze to my face in the winter cold.

"Quinn, please!" He tries again, but I'm already out of the woods and into the backyard. "I didn't want to scare you. Can we please just talk?"

"Talk!?" I just about squawk. "You want to fucking talk now?" I shake my head. "Leave me the fuck alone, Beckett. You're better off just leaving the journal alone too. If it's not there... it's probably gone."

He grabs my arm and I scream. "Quinn." He pleads softly despite my shrieks like I'm being fucking murdered by the ghost of the Zodiac Killer. "Please." He offers gently. "I just want to talk. You... even if you don't have the journal, you know what was in it. Can we please just talk?"

I yank my arm free of him. "No."

Chapter Fourteen

Quinn

Beckett has stopped by no less than ten times today asking for me and every time Bridget slams the door in his face which I actually quite appreciate. So when yet another knock sounds at the door, no one even bothers to leave the kitchen to go check.

Caleb and the kids are all watching some brainrot TV show in the living room. I don't know what it is, but it's loud enough that I keep hearing it in the kitchen over the Christmas music.

Adriane is sitting at the kitchen island next to my dad, both of whom are helping with cooking intermittently when we ask them to, but mostly Adriane is reading and my dad is playing on his tablet. Honestly that's fine though between Bridget, Ashley, and I we have dinner pretty much covered. We'll make enough tonight for left overs for everyone to take home tomorrow and then just cook the breakfast casseroles in the mornings and food is covered til the twenty sixth.

"He's being very–" Ashley starts.

"Annoying?" Bridget cuts her off.

"I was going to say persistent." Ashley shrugs.

"Annoying is more accurate." I grumble.

He keeps calling and texting me. It got to the point where I decided to just leave my phone upstairs so I didn't have to feel it constantly buzzing in my pocket, which I'm especially frustrated about because I was trying to have a conversation with Madison. I'm sure that my phone is still ringing off the hook. I wouldn't be surprised if it hasn't vibrated right off the guest bed.

The doorbell rings again and this time, my dad gets to his feet. "Alright, that's enough. Time to put the fear of god in him."

"Dad." I sigh. "That's not–"

"Do you have any idea how many boys I had to scare off when you two were in high school?" He asks on a chuckle. "Won't be the first time I've had to shoo Beckett off our porch."

My eyes go wide, considering briefly how different my life would have been had my dad let Beckett in when I was a teenager, but I guess it doesn't really matter since he didn't.

Bridget smiles as my dad heads down the hallway towards the front door. "Good, maybe now we can actually enjoy Christmas Eve."

I swallow and stop cutting the potatoes I was working on. I creep quietly towards the hallway, stopping at the bend, but close enough that I can hear the conversation about to transpire.

"Turn that off for a second." My dad says to Caleb with a wave of his hand.

Caleb grabs the remote and pauses the TV. The kids all boo, annoyed at the stimulation loss, but Caleb just says, "Who wants to go make snowmen?" And starts grabbing the kids stuff to go outside. He runs them towards the backdoor with their things much faster than I've ever seen him herd the kids before. Once they are all out of the room my dad opens the door.

"Bridget–" Beckett starts and immediately freezes when he sees my dad. "Mr. O'Brady, I–"

"Leave Quinn alone." My dad says, cutting straight to the chase. "We had this conversation when you were a teenager, I don't know why we're having it again now." His voice is stern in a way that I've never heard before, terrifyingly so.

Beckett shifts back on his feet.

"She lives in New York," My dad's voice has a twinge of sadness at those words, but he pushes on, "And she loves it there. She isn't about to move back to Vermont for you."

Beckett chews on his lip, crossing his arms over his chest. "You don't understand." He replies.

"And I don't intend to." My father counters. "Unless you plan on moving to New York to be with her you have no business pulling her heart around for a couple weeks while she's here. It's not fair to her."

"It's more complicated than that." Beckett says, but I can tell he's starting to shrink, I can see him losing the confidence he had when the door first opened.

"I don't care." My dad's back is to me so I can't see the look in his eyes, but whatever it is, Beckett takes a step backwards. "Quinn told you she didn't want to talk to you. Bridget told you Quinn didn't want to talk to you. Now I'm telling you that Quinn doesn't want to talk to you."

Beckett's jaw ticks, but he doesn't reply.

"It's Christmas Eve." My dad pushes. "I'm sure you have somewhere that you could be instead of here harassing my daughter. And if I see you on my property again I won't bother calling the police. I have plenty of shovels in the back shed." Then my dad slams the door without another word.

I'm shaking a little more than I wish I was. I might be pissed at Beckett but I really don't like the idea of him getting hurt.

"Heard all that, Quinn?" My dad asks, turning around to look at where I was hiding.

I step out from behind the wall with a nod. "Yeah."

He nods too and turns to head down the hallway. "Take however long you need." He says as he passes me, giving me a quick pat on the shoulder before heading back into the kitchen.

I on the other hand head to the front windows. I get there just in time to watch Beckett take a look back at the house and climb into his truck with his jaw clenched. I put my hand up to the window and I have half a mind to go after him, but I don't.

Honestly, I hadn't really considered everything my dad said. I am going back to New York. Whatever this fling is between Beckett and I, it can't be serious because we both have our own lives in two completely different states. I had been so consumed with everything from our past, that I didn't consider that Beckett and I have no future.

Beckett's truck pulls back down the driveway slowly. I watch every second until he pulls out onto the road and drives away. It takes a few minutes before I leave the window, almost like I'm waiting for him to come back but I know he won't.

When I head back into the kitchen, whatever discussion was being had in low voices a moment later stops. It makes me feel like a pariah. Everyone is staring at me and I really don't know how to handle that.

I head back over to the cutting board I abandoned and start working on the potatoes again, but the eyes don't stop. For a few minutes I keep my head down and everyone goes back to work, but then Bridget taps me on the shoulder.

"Quinn?" Bridget asks softly.

"Mhm?" I peek my head up and only then realize I'm crying. I set the knife down before wiping at my eyes. "It's just the damn onion that Ash is cutting." I say, waving them off, but the lie is obvious.

"Quinn, maybe you should take a break." Ashley says softly. "Bridget and I can finish cutting the potatoes."

I'm tempted to try and tell her that I'm fine. I'm tempted to keep cooking and just pretend like nothing is wrong. I really don't want to show how much that this is affecting me. He shouldn't be affecting me.

"Yeah." I mutter, fighting the urge to run up the stairs and away from them, away from everyone, because what I really want to do is run to *him*. And I can't fucking do that.

Didn't I just hate this man yesterday? Why is he confusing me to the point where I'm just about losing my mind? Something about wanting what I can't have, I'm sure.

In the end, I do head upstairs, forcing my steps to slow. As I make my way into the guest room I just about throw myself at my phone, scrambling for it on the bed desperate to see if he's texted me or tried to call me since he left.

There are a slew of older texts from before he talked to my dad, most of them begging me to talk to him, a few of them vaguely sexual, several of them explicitly sexual, and one from a minute ago, but not from his actual number.

Unknown: You have until midnight to text me back, or you will see just how far I am willing to go to see you.

I stare down at the lock screen waiting to see if he will text me again. After a second I open the unknown text thread and the text bubbles I expect to start popping up don't. His threat looms in the air over me and I don't really know what to make of it. He didn't really promise anything, but that's almost worse, because that means he could *do anything.*

I keep waiting for text bubbles and I'm so focused on that, when the knock sounds at my door my hands jolt and the phone drops to the bed while I jump up so quickly I might as well have flown. "Yes?" I ask, a part of me scared it's Beckett.

Bridget comes inside the room, closing the door behind her. "I need to tell you something." She says chewing on her lip. She moves to sit down on the bed and I sit back down too. "I followed you and Beckett yesterday."

I grimace. "Why?"

"To see if you were going where I thought you were going." She answers, her hands starting to play nervously in the sheets. "But that's not what I need to tell you."

I wait on baited breath and Bridget seems to draw it out like she's scared of how I'm going to take whatever she says next.

"I know where the journal is."

Chapter Fifteen

Quinn

"Quinn," My homeroom teacher says, pulling me aside as I'm about to leave the classroom to head to chemistry. "I got a note this morning to have you report to Principal Ericson's office."

I blink, confused, "Did it say why?"

She shakes her head. "No. Just to have you go before first period."

"Okay." I nod, swallowing the nausea rising in my stomach.

I pad my way down the stairs towards the first floor offices. Other students flood in around me, but I just try to keep my head down. I don't really feel like talking to someone, but life is never that simple.

Alexa stops me in the hallway. "Quinn, are you okay?"

I look up at her and scoff as hard as I possibly can which I'm sure came out wildly exaggerated. "Now you fucking ask? I've been trying to text you since... since..." I take a deep shaky breath. "You haven't asked about me this whole time. You've treated me like a social pariah."

"I know." Alexa whispers. "I'm sorry. I should have texted you. I should have reached out, I just... After Josh and I started talking I didn't know what to say."

I chew on my lip. "And that just makes all of this worse. I don't... I really don't know what you've been thinking. Do you not see how violent he is? He's not a safe person Alexa."

"Quinn." She offers softly, but I just start to storm off. I think I'm going to get away from her too but then she grabs my arm and yanks me down a quieter hallway. "Look, what happened to Lila..." My teeth grit. "She didn't understand him like I do."

"I don't want to hear this."

"Quinn, it's different." Alexa pleads. "Josh and I have been friends since grade school. We

have a special connection. You have to under-stand that it's different."

"Why because you actually let him fuck you?" I hiss. "What do you think would have happened to you if you didn't? Do you think you'd be in the same grave next to Lila?"

"Stop." Alexa growls. "That's not what happened. Josh told me the truth. That's why I haven't been hanging around you, Quinn. You always fucking lie."

"The truth?" I blink at her confused. "What truth did he tell you exactly?"

Alexa shifts on her feet softly before admitting, "Lila chose to kill herself." And the second the words leave Alexa's mouth my eyes go wide in shock. That's the story he's been telling people? "She asked him to not leave her alone while she did it and he didn't want people to think he was responsible."

I stand there frozen for a second trying to process what the fuck she just said. I know what I saw, I saw Josh kill Lila, not just the aftermath, not just blood, I saw him actively kill her. There is no doubt in my mind what happened, but his story... it's more convincing than I wish it was.

Lila had struggled with depression for a while, the thought of her killing herself isn't so far off base as to be impossible. Honestly, even I might have believed it if I hadn't seen the truth with my own two eyes.

"That's not what happened." I breathe out, trying to figure out how to put a sentence together after the insane thing that Alexa just dropped on me. "That's not... That's not what happened." I just repeat, not knowing what else to say.

"Then what did happen, Quinn?" Alexa asks. "Becuase from what I heard, you and Beckett have both been awfully quiet about the whole thing to everyone except the police. You know it's a crime to lie to the police right?"

"I'm not a liar." I growl.

She scoffs. "I'm more inclined to trust Josh over you and little miss easy way out."

"I'm done with this conversation." I start to storm off and hear stomps behind me going in the other direction.

Alexa huffs, "Believe me, I'm fucking done too. We are not friends anymore! Lose my number, bitch!"

"GLADLY!" I shriek at her and if I wasn't in trouble before I definitely fucking am now be-

cause a handful of teachers have peeked their heads out of their classrooms to see the commotion. I just turn heel and run down the hallway towards the principal's office.

For better or worse, I make it down to the office without further interruption or confrontation. My hands dig into my palm as I walk through the open doors to the front office.

I already know Mr. Ericson wants to talk to me about his son. I already have an idea of how this conversation is going to go and I think I would prefer to go back to arguing with Alexa. At least arguing with Alexa I can speak my mind without fear of getting expelled.

This is going to be rough.

"Miss, O'Brady." The receptionist smiles brightly. "Mr. Ericson's office is third door on the left." She says pointing back down the hallway, apparently not having any idea why I'm here since she's being so warm to me and not looking at me with the pity I've gotten very used to recently.

When your best friend dies everyone treats you with kid gloves, honestly it's been really annoying. I know I'm not fine, but everyone treating me differently is just reminding me *how not fine I am. I would give anything for things to be normal again, but I'm not sure I know what normal looks like now without Lila.*

Lila and I talked every day. We texted constantly when we weren't around each other. I'm the only person who knows what's in her journal...

I miss her.

I walk down the hallway and my hand hesitates to knock on the door, but it doesn't matter because Josh's dad sees me through the window. "Come in, Ms. O'Brady." Mr. Ericson says with a wave.

His dark brown hair is starting to gray. His suit is wrinkled, between that and the bags under his eyes he looks... tired. Really tired. And honestly I am too after everything that's happened.

The door creaks as I turn the handle and push into the room. I try to leave it open so someone else can hear whatever conversation is about to happen, "You can close the door." I recognize immediately that it's not a request, so I do.

"Please, take a seat." He says, gesturing to the soft chairs that sit across from his desk.

Reluctantly I do, wanting more than anything to just run from the room screaming, but that's not an option. I mean, I guess it is, but I don't need people thinking I've lost it more than I actually have.

"I want to talk to you about your college applications." He hums, grabbing out a few folders and passing one to me. "I have two letters here, that I could send out to colleges about you and I just wanted you to proof read them and tell me which one you like better."

I take the folder and quickly peruse both letters. The first one is a glowing recommendation, nicer than I have honestly earned with his signature across the bottom. The second is harsher; it makes me look not just bad, but borderline criminal.

I swallow, but pass him the nice one. "This one."

He nods. "Yes, well it's nice when people say good things about you, isn't it?"

I nod.

"So I think it's important that you only say nice things about my son." His voice turns gruff as he takes back the letters from me.

"I know what I saw, Mr. Ericson."

He tsks softly. "Do you, Ms. O'Brady?" He holds up the letter that slanders my name up and down the page. "Because this letter knows what it thinks about you. And I think it would be best for everyone if what you think you know about my son and what this letter thinks it knows about you, both went away."

"I can't do that." I shake my head. "They... they've already asked me to testify."

"You're young." He says. "And you have such a bright future ahead of you. My son does too. Don't you think it's important that those futures stay intact?"

"This isn't fair." I try not to shout, but I want to. My voice comes out clipped, fighting to keep my volume down.

Mr. Ericson sets the letter down on his desk. "It's not. And I am sorry about that, Quinn." He says earnestly. "But at the end of the day, I have to do what's best for my family. And I think you should do what's best for yourself."

I chew on my lip, watching him and not knowing how to react.

"You don't need to testify, Quinn." He pushes. "I'm not asking you to lie. You can just recant your statement and refuse to testify. It was dark. You didn't know what you saw

and you were confused. You didn't have to see anything."

I swallow hard. "But..."

"Please, Quinn." Mr. Ericson says softly. "I want to help you. Let me send out this letter recommending you to every Ivy League in the country. Let me get you out of this town and somewhere better. There's somewhere better, Quinn."

"I..." I shake my head. "I don't know. What... What about Lila?" If I listened, if I did this, I'd be letting her killer walk. I'd be letting her name be slandered. I'd be letting everyone just believe she did this to herself when I know better.

"Lila would want what's best for you, Quinn." Mr. Ericson encourages. "She wanted to get out of here. She wanted to leave this town. Do it for her. Let her memory live on in you."

I nod. "Okay." I whisper softly.

"Good." He takes the second letter, the one that would have condemned me, and puts it in the shredder. "I'll send these out as soon as you're off the witness list."

"Am I free to go?" I ask.

He nods. "Yes. But if you needed to make a call you can do that here." He says pushing his phone towards me. He wants me to call the police now...

I hesitate, I consider Lila, I consider Beck, and most of all I consider if I'm really doing the right thing here... And in the end, I make the wrong decision.

I pick up the phone and dial the non-emergency police number. An operator picks up. "Hi, I would like to recant a statement I made."

Chapter Sixteen

Quinn

I watch my phone, staring at the little hand moving on the clock app as it spins around to eleven fifty nine. I don't know if I'm expecting him to just text me or show up or what the fuck ever he is going to do exactly at twelve, but the hand turns over and its midnight.

I hold my breath waiting for whatever I'm waiting for and... nothing happens. Another minute passes on the clock and there's no foreboding text, no knock at my front door, nothing.

Well that was rather anticlimactic.

I snuggle into the couch with my laptop and blanket. The living room is quiet with everyone back home now and my dad asleep. Bridget and Adriane will be back in the morning, but right now the house is peaceful.

My tea warms my stomach as I watch the fireplace crackle, a real one this time, and the anxiety of a few moments prior starts to fade. A half hour passes and still all is quiet on the night before Christmas.

I start reading the next chapter of Madison's book and trying my absolute fucking hardest to focus on that and not think about Beckett, but it's late and my mind wanders to him anyways. It's not helping that this chapter I'm reading is a fucking sex scene. I keep picturing the MMC as Beckett even though they look nothing alike.

I try to keep an eye on the words, I try to do my job and keep objective, looking for better wording suggestions and grammar errors, but I can't. Fuck it, I'll reread this chapter later when I'm not horny out of my mind.

I slip my hand between my legs, under my leggings and the second my fingers find the tender bundle of nerves I have to stifle a moan. My eyes scan over the words in the chapter as I try to keep my breathing steady. At least I'm covered by the blanket on the off chance my dad comes downstairs I can feign innocence.

My eyes are so focused on the chapter that I don't pay any mind to the headlights that come through the front window. I see them out of the corner of my eyes but they don't register, I chalk it up to the porch lights or something, not really caring with my thoughts full of Beckett. I only truly consider that someone is here when a few minutes later I hear the front door handle start to rattle.

I jerk my hand free, wiping off my fingers on the blanket urgently, but I don't have enough time to actually get away from whoever is about to come in because the lock gets picked too quickly.

The door is pushed open quietly and I see Beckett standing there, covered in snow and not wearing a fucking shirt. He smirks at me, "Starting without me?" He has on a Santa hat, black suspenders, and red Santa pants and is fucking holding a couple presents (just to complete the look I'm sure).

My eyes go wide trying to figure out what the fuck to do with the hot Santa in front of me who just broke into my house. "You saw?" I ask sheepishly.

He nods, closing the door behind him. Beck walks over to the tree. It's illuminated with colorful Christmas lights, wrapping around gently intermingled with silver garland. Ornaments found throughout the years are scattered on the branches, most of which I recognize from childhood. There is tinsel tossed haphazardly on the branches and loads of candy canes.

He sets down the two small boxes underneath of it. "Well my work here is done." He comes to stand over me, his arms resting comfortably on the back of the couch as he looks down at me. "Got any milk and cookies for me, firebug?"

I shake my head.

He sighs and reaches down to my chin to tilt my head up. "And here I thought you had been a good girl this year."

"I have been." I rush to answer.

Beck tsks softly. "But you didn't leave me my offerings," He shrugs, "Maybe I'll just take the presents back," His hand caresses my face softly, "Unless we can work something else out."

I nod feverishly. "Yes."

My whole world is consumed by his smirk. The chill in my bones from the cold is immediately heated as I stare up at him with wide eyes trying desperately to put two thoughts together.

He leans down to whisper in my ear and the way his breath brushes up against my skin makes my toes curl. "Do you want me to be naughty or nice, Quinn?"

"Naughty." I breathe out.

Beck grabs my laptop and closes it. He pulls the blanket off me and with neither him or the blanket's warmth I feel the chill from the cool air of the house again. Snow cascades down outside the window filling the view of the porch.

He drops to his knees and the sight is beautiful. Beck pulls me to the edge of the couch, pulling down my leggings so they are around my ankles before he spreads my legs. His head dives between my legs without a second thought and he starts licking softly up and down my folds.

I grumble a little, wanting more than that. "Please, lick my clit please." I beg on an exhale.

"I was getting to that." He mutters into my pussy, but he obliges me anyways. Beck's tongue finds my center and he licks it slowly, deliberately like he's trying to fuck with me.

"Beck." I furrow my brow, trying to push myself into his beard, but the man has the fucking nerve to grab my legs and pin me down to the couch.

He licks at me a few more times before pulling away. "I was going to use those fingers for something else, but since you can't seem to behave, maybe that's not an option." He shrugs.

"No, please." I whisper. "I'll behave."

"Will you?" He counters.

I shake my head.

"That's what I thought." He pushes up off the ground and walks over to the tree. Beck grabs one of the presents he brought in and hands it to me. "Open this."

I take the golden package out of his hand and eye it skeptically. "What is it?"

"A box." He answers and my brows pinch. "You have to open it, Quinn. I can't just tell you. That's not how it works."

My fingers drift to the tape on the sides and with my nails I slice it off. I carefully pull the wrapping paper open and see a plain black box.

Beck chuckles. "Of course you are one of those."

"What?" I huff.

"Just the way you open presents." He shrugs. "It's very neat. Most people just rip into it with reckless abandon."

"That's messy." I respond, taking the lid off the black box. I've seen enough sex toys to recognize immediately what was inside, a small silicone egg vibrator. I chew on my lip as Beck plucks the vibrator out of the box.

"Lean back, Quinn." He purrs, as he picks up the remote next to it.

I do as I'm told.

Beck pulls me closer to the edge again and rubs the egg up and down my slit. "You're so wet, Quinn." He purrs as he pushes the egg inside of me.

I wait on baited breath for him to turn it on but he doesn't. Instead he gets back down on the ground between my legs. He pins them back down and goes back to licking my center. This time his strokes are less languid, his tongue pushes with a need in long deliberate motions.

I moan, my head kicking back.

The fireplace crackles, the wind whistles through the house, and the only other sound is Beck between my legs. The only light to see by is the tree and the soft glow of the moon off the snow outside.

This continues for a few minutes before he says, "Think anyone would mind if I stole the garland off the tree and used it to tie your hands together?" He chuckles between my legs.

"If they do, I don't care." I moan.

He finally turns on the egg then and a soft buzz makes me jump. "Stay still." He purrs, pushing back up to his feet.

Staying still is a much taller order than I think he realizes because he turns the egg up another level and it's hard not to twitch.

Beck starts to carefully unwrap some of the silver garland from the tree, making sure not to disturb the rest of the decorations which is kind of impressive since the garland is in the middle of the tree. He gets a smaller piece free that's still at least ten feet long or so.

He walks back over to me and takes my hands, putting them together before wrapping the center of the garland around them a few times and tying it off. Then he takes the other two ends and ties my knees open on both sides. All the while I'm shaking from the vibrator shoved up my pussy.

"You haven't stayed very still." He growls, slapping my pussy softly.

"Wrap a vibrating cock ring around your dick and then you try to stay still." I hiss back, but that's clearly not the right response because he slaps my pussy again.

"Maybe another time." Beck smirks. He continues to stand over me and his fingers find my clit and start massaging feverishly. Before he was playing around, now he's trying to make me cum, the difference is clear.

I grind on his fingers as he works me trying to help him get me over the edge. It doesn't take long with how he's moving. It's clear Beck knows what he's doing and whoever gave him that experience, their loss is my gain.

My head starts to cloud and I feel the orgasm building between my legs. I let out a moan that's just a little too loud and one of Beck's hands shoots up to cover my mouth.

He shushes me and for some reason that's what does it because I find myself finishing immediately, biting my lip hard behind his hand trying to keep myself quiet. "That's a good girl." He purrs, as he pulls the vibrator free of my pussy and turns it off.

Beck doesn't give me time to rest though, instead he pulls me off the couch and brings me down to the bearskin rug. He bends me over the sofa, my hands forced upwards onto the seat so my legs are stuck open before he drops down behind me.

I'm panting from my orgasm as I turn to see him pull his pants down behind me. His huge cock is rock fucking hard and he starts to tease me, rubbing up and down my entrance. I try to push back on him, but he holds me firm.

"You want me, Quinn?" He asks, his voice almost as ragged as I feel.

"Yes." I moan.

"Then stop ignoring my calls." He growls as he pushes inside of me. "Stop dodging my texts." He strokes into me hard and I fight the urge to scream. "Stop hiding when I knock on your door."

I nod.

He groans softly as he starts to fuck me into the couch. "If you want to see me, Quinn," He snakes his hand between my legs and starts massaging my too tender clit. "You can't keep letting your family scare me off." His fingers stop. "Apologize."

"I'm sorry." I breathe out without even considering it. I don't know if I truly am though and apparently he must not believe me because he pulls his hand back away from me.

Beck keeps his rhythm steady. "If I wasn't worried about being too loud, I would be spanking you for lying to me." He strokes in harder. "Since you're being naughty, maybe I need to take your other present back."

I don't know what the present is, but I find myself wanting it anyways, especially after the first one. "Please, no. I'm sorry I lied."

He does seem to accept that apology. "Why don't you want to see me, Quinn?"

"You want to have this conversation, now?" I ask incredulously.

I feel his shrug behind me. "I guess it can wait." He purrs. Then he fucking groans and the sound makes my eyes roll into the back of my head with pleasure. Beck grabs my hair by the base and pulls me back onto him with just the right amount of force that it's more pleasurable than painful.

My sweater bunches up around me in odd ways as I'm tugged repeatedly down onto his cock. The wind whistles through the windows again and I'm thankful for Beck's warmth.

I put my head down into the couch to stifle my moans as I twitch around him. I squeeze his length in time with his motions and Becket lets out another groan.

"Fuck, Quinn."

"Beck." I respond in kind.

He pushes in and finishes between my legs with a soft moaning growl. "Fuck, you feel so damned good, firebug." He pulls out of me and readjusts his pants before starting to untie me.

Once the garland is undone, he goes to put it back on the tree while I fix my leggings. "I..." My words catch in my throat trying to figure out what to say after something like that.

"Now can we talk about why you're dodging my phone calls?" Beckett asks.

I recover quickly then, sliding up onto the couch and sheltering myself back under the blanket. "I don't... I don't want to talk about that."

He comes to sit down on the couch across from me. He puts his hands on his knees and leans forwards, but I appreciate that he's giving me space. "Why not?"

"Because this isn't real." I shrug softly. "This is just some fling that both of us will remember fondly and maybe fall back into next year when I'm back for the holidays again if we are both still single."

His jaw ticks. "Is that really what you think of this?"

I chew on my lip. "Could it be anything more?" I ask genuinely. "My dad is right, my life is in New York and yours–"

He cuts me off. "Can be wherever you are."

"Do you mean that?" My wide eyes stare at him in disbelief.

"Quinn, I have nothing keeping me here." He says. "My father left, my mother and sister are both gone. And as it turns out, there are fires in New York City last I checked."

I chuckle. "Well and if there's not you can make some."

"Exactly." He smiles like it's not quite a joke.

"Do you really mean that?"

"That I can start fires anywhere?" He asks. "Yeah, I mean most places have lighter fluid."

I look at him deadpan. "I mean that you'd move to New York for me."

He gets up off his couch and comes to sit on mine. Beckett takes my hands in his. "Quinn, I've been in love with you as far back as I can remember and there is literally nothing keeping me here. If you're not ready for us to take it that fast I can get my own place, but yeah, I'd move to New York for you. And honestly a little for me too, I kinda hate it here."

"I do too."

Chapter Seventeen

Beckett

Quinn let me stay the night over at her parents place, in her bedroom, high school me would have lost his ever loving shit if he knew about this. I woke up much earlier than she did but I just waited on my phone for her. I didn't want to take my chances of running into her dad alone. I'm still scared Mitchell might kill me and while I could defend myself, Quinn would probably kill me herself if I hurt her dad.

She's beautiful when she's sleeping. Her curling red hair swirling around her freckle covered face. She tosses softly but she doesn't snore in her sleep which feels rather intimate to know.

It's not until after nine that Quinn wakes up but considering she didn't fall asleep until almost three in the morning I'm inclined to give her a pass on that. She stretches and turns over to look at me with a soft smile. "Hi." She whispers.

"Hi." I respond in kind.

"Merry Christmas." She says, sitting upwards in the bed and watching me with careful eyes. She looks cautious, like she thinks I'm going to disappear at any moment.

"Merry Christmas." I lean in to kiss her and when I do she melts into me. The kiss is full of passion and need. Her arms go around my shoulders quickly as she leans into me with her soft lips eating up mine.

Quinn moans a little into the kiss and I can feel myself getting hard in my boxers. I'm so glad I had a change of clothes in the truck because while the sexy Santa may have done it for Quinn I have a feeling her family isn't going to appreciate it as much as she did.

After a second I pull away from her and she has the biggest smile spreading across her face. "That's one hell of a way to wake up." She muses softly to herself. "I think I could get used to that."

"I could too." I smirk at her.

Quinn pushes off the bed in her Christmas pajamas, a pair of red and green plaid pants and a t-shirt that reads, *Kiss Me I've Been Naughty*. I'm inclined to take her up on that offer, even if I did just kiss her a second ago. She runs a hand through her hair. "Coffee?"

"Yeah." I respond, climbing out from under the covers and following her downstairs.

Her dad sits on the counter, "Merry Christmas, Quinn." He says, when he turns his head and sees me his smile turns into a grimace. "Didn't I tell you to fuck off?"

"You told me to leave Quinn alone if she didn't want to talk to me. She wants to talk to me." I try not to smirk in *fuck you* and remember that this might be my father in law one day so it's best to stay on his good side.

"Mhm." He huffs. "And how many times did you have to call her to make her talk to you?" He challenges.

"Dad." Quinn chides like she's the adult in this situation despite being the youngest one in the room. "He's fine. I want him to be here."

"Quinn–" Mitchell starts again.

"I said it's fine." She insists and it comes out strong, not like that of a petulant teenager like I was expecting, but rather the voice of a woman who knows what she wants, and what she wants is me. I fight the urge to smirk.

I make my way over to the coffee pot that's sitting on the counter. Quinn passes me a couple cups, one for each of us, and I fill them both. "Room for cream?" I ask her.

Quinn nods. "Yeah."

I can feel her father staring daggers at me even if I'm not looking at him. "She said I was fine." I tell him, turning back around and taking a sip of the coffee.

"That doesn't mean I like you."

I shrug. "Quinn likes me."

"Dad, you don't like any of the guys I've dated." Quinn sighs, moving to pour some creamer into her coffee. "So you'll excuse me if I don't care if you like this one."

I wrap an arm around Quinn's waist, pulling her into my chest. "We can stay at my place tonight, if you want." I whisper to her. "I need to start packing anyways."

She chuckles softly. "I think I'd like that."

"I'm going into the living room to wait for your sister. At least her partner is someone I like." Mitchell grumbles as he takes his coffee and moseys out of the kitchen.

"I'm sorry about him." Quinn leans back into me taking a sip of her coffee.

I shrug. "It's not your fault, he'll come around." I don't know if that's true but that feels like the kind of thing you say to your girlfriend when her father doesn't like you. Is she my girlfriend?

"Hey, what is this?" I spin her around to face me. "What are we to each other? We talked about where this was going last night, but we didn't label it."

She shrugs then. "What do you want us to be?"

What I want us to be and what wouldn't scare her off are two very different things. I would elope with her this afternoon if she asked me to, but I have a feeling that's too big of a step for her. "Let's start with boyfriend and girlfriend? We can go from there?"

"Yeah, let's start there." Quinn smiles.

There is a ring at the doorbell and Quinn turns her head. "Bridget probably won't be thrilled to see you either." She chews on her lip.

"They'll get used to me." I tell her.

"Or we could spend most of the rest of my time here at your place and then not talk to them when we're in Manhattan." Quinn suggests and I question how much it's a joke.

"I think I like that plan." I smile back at her. "But I do think they are going to want to see you for at least the rest of today considering it is Christmas."

She sighs. "Ugh. Yeah, probably." She runs a hand through her hair, taking a sip of her coffee in tandem, and marches out of the kitchen with a kinda steadiness that's just insanely fucking hot. If her family wasn't in the other room I'd grab her, pin her against the wall, and lick every inch of her until she was screaming at me to eat her out.

I follow behind her, knowing I'm in for an uphill battle if I ever want my future in-laws to like me even slightly. They all used to like me when I was younger. It wasn't until everything with Lila and the trial that things changed. Our families used to be pretty close.

"Quinn!" Bridget smiles and then she sees me and does the same thing her dad did. "Why is he here?" She glares at me.

"He's my boyfriend." Quinn states plainly. "He had nowhere else to be. I invited him. He looks hot in a Santa hat. Do you need more reasons?"

"What happened to, he's bad news and that you were going to stay away from him?" Bridget argues.

"What happened to, I'm an adult and can do what I want?" Quinn bickers back, this time seeming a lot less sure of herself than she was before.

Bridget eyes me up and down. "He can't be here." She says plainly.

Adriane pushes past her. "I don't care about this, I'm going to sit down." She waves politely at me. "Merry Christmas, Beckett."

"Merry Christmas." I smile back at her and move to sit on the couch that is currently vacant.

Quinn follows behind me and just about sits in my fucking lap, likely to prove a point to her sister. "He's staying."

"Not if you're going to sit like that, he's not." Her father says, his tone leaving no room for argument. "And here I thought you were never going to have that rebellious phase, I guess thirty one is the new seventeen."

Quinn moves off my lap and sits next to me. She folds her arms over her chest, annoyed. "If you all can't respect him, I will just fucking leave. I don't mind catching a flight home on Christmas Day." She warns.

Bridget and Mitchell look between each other but it's Adriane who finally speaks. "Beckett, can you keep mostly quiet?" I nod and she nods back. "Great, then he's not hurting anything as long as he just sits there. Ash and the kids are going to be here any second, do you all really want them to see you arguing?"

Another set of glances is exchanged among everyone before Bridget finally sits down between Adriane and her father. "Fine." Bridget grumbles. "Merry Christmas, asshole."

I smile but I'm sure it's more like a sneer. "Merry Christmas, Bridget."

Chapter Eighteen

Quinn

How the hell do I tell him I know where the journal is? And I've come to the conclusion that I have to fucking tell him. It's not an option to just pretend I don't know. This man is packing up his whole life and moving to New York for me, he deserves the truth.

Beckett's house is on the smaller side, just one story, but he has a crap ton of land on all sides of him. His bedroom is painted a dark gray, between that and the blackout curtains, it's completely dark in here when he turns the lights off. It's kinda nice. My apartment is all white walls and brightness.

His mattress is on the ground which feels very early twenties as opposed to mid thirties. It's pushed into the corner with a dresser across from the long end. Atop the dresser is an assortment of gaming consoles with a TV mounted above it. His ceiling has mirror panels over the bed which made last night more than just a little interesting.

Beckett comes back into the room holding a cup of coffee. I take it and ruffle through the blankets in the dark looking for my phone. "What time is it?"

"Almost noon." He leans against the wall next to the bed. "I figured we could get some boxes today and start packing."

I kinda just stare at him for a second and take a sip of my coffee, thankful he remembered to put creamer in it... and that he even had creamer in the first place. "Are you sure about this?" I ask him, running a hand through my hair. "This is a big change and I feel like you're rushing into this."

"Quinn, I thought we talked about this?"

I nod. "We did. I just... I'm scared you're going to wake up one day and feel like you made a mistake."

"I don't know how to assure you that I'm not." Beckett says, coming to sit down on the bed. My nose twitches and he looks at me like he's analyzing something. "What are you not telling me?"

I shake my head. "Nothing, I..." But my voice squeaks and I immediately know I'm caught in the lie. I sigh and chew on my lip. "It's..."

"Do you have a boyfriend back in New York?"

"No, definitely not that." I take another sip of my coffee, trying to put some time together for me to figure out what to say next. "Bridget... She told me where the journal is now."

He freezes. "What?"

"Apparently when I hid it all those years ago, Bridget saw." I start to explain. "And-"

"How long have you known where it was?" His tone is gruff, full of frustration I can tell he's trying to tamp down.

"A few days." I admit softly. "She told me after we went looking for the journal. She saw where we went and knew what we were looking for."

Beckett adjusts his jaw. "You should have told me sooner."

"I know." I look up at him with soft eyes. "But for what it's worth, I'm telling you now."

Beckett takes a second, a deep breath rattling through him, clearly trying to calm himself down. "I've been looking for that journal for over a decade. I've never been as close as I was the other day and... Then I scared the shit out of you and you almost never talked to me again."

"I don't... I don't think it's worth it anymore." Beckett mutters. "Maybe it's time I just let Lila's memory be at peace."

I stare at him with wide eyes. "Seriously?"

Beckett nods. "Since I lost the lead on the journal the other day, I've felt more at peace than I have in a long time. I think Lila's memory deserves that too. I don't know if it's fair for me to keep dragging her ghost around with me just because I never moved on."

I blink at him, trying to figure out if he's lost his mind. "You were just torturing me over this thing less than a fucking week ago, and *now* you're just over it?"

"No." He answers. "I'm not over it. But I'm tired and I don't feel like going on another wild goose chase for something that may or may not be at the end of it."

A moment of pause passes between the two of us and I can't help but feel like my head just got spun around in ten different directions before being screwed back on straight. "What?"

Beckett kisses me on the cheek. "What I want is you, Quinn." He whispers into my ear. "I want us to be together. And most of all I want to start living in the future. Not the past." He pushes up off the bed. "So get dressed and we'll go get some boxes."

"All I have here are my pajamas." I chuckle.

He walks over to his dresser and pulls open one of the drawers. Beckett tosses me a black hoodie. "Here, this will work with your pajama pants." He smirks at me.

I take his hoodie, pulling it over my head and can't help but feel like maybe this is the start of a new chapter.

"Are you sure you don't want to know?" I ask him *again* as we load the boxes from the store into the back of his truck.

"Yes." He sighs exasperatedly. "I'm sure I don't want to know."

"But..." I drag out the word. "How can you really be sure? How do you know you know you don't want to know?"

"Quinn," Beckett turns to me, resting a hand on the bed of his truck with an exasperated look, "That sentence was nonsense, and I'm fine." He promises. "I don't want to know. I *do* want to move to New York. And most of all I want you to stop asking the same questions a hundred times like you're waiting for me to change my answer."

I nod. "Okay." We finish loading the last of the boxes into the back of the truck, he goes to the drivers side but I stop him. "Can I drive?"

He kinda looks at me, debating if he thinks that's a good idea or not. "Yeah, okay." He passes me the keys, I smile but he grimaces. "Please just don't fucking crash."

"I know how to drive." I grumble.

"You live in New York." He pushes back. "I'm sure you know how, I just question how much you actually do it."

I roll my eyes at him. "I drive plenty." But he gives me the look that he caught the lie so I don't know why I tried. "Okay fine, really only when I'm here, but I still know how."

He sighs and climbs into the passenger side despite this conversation not being the best indicator of my driving abilities.

Madison and I agreed he could stay with us until he found a place, which shouldn't be too hard once he sells his house. Him and I think that moving in together is too much, but there are apartments open in my building that he can more than afford.

Is this all moving too fast?

Probably, but I don't know if I should be stopping it or leaning into it. Moving for someone feels like such a big step and while I'm not really giving anything up for him, he's giving up a lot for me.

"What if I always feel like I owe you?" My eyes scan the road looking for the turn off.

He glances over at me. "What do you mean?"

"This is a big thing you're doing for me." My thumb plays on the steering wheel. "How can I ever do something like that for you?"

His jaw ticks as he seems to think about how to respond. The waiting is causing my stomach to drop and I'm sure I'm going to throw up on the spot. "Quinn, relationships aren't transactional like that. You don't have to do anything for me."

"Yeah, I do." I mutter. I had been undecided up until that point if I was going to turn or not, but now... now I have to. I move into the left lane as the light starts to turn red and slow down.

"Where are you going?" He asks, confused. "My place is straight."

"Josh and Alexa's," I answer softly.

A long pause passes through the car, long enough that the light turns green. "Why?" I can tell he's swallowing his anger. "Why are we going there?" His voice comes out clipped.

"To get the journal back." I answer simply.

"Josh has the journal?" His hands curl in his lap, no longer able to hide the anger. "Why wouldn't he just destroy it?"

I shake my head. "Josh doesn't have the journal."

"Alexa?" He asks.

I nod. "Apparently Bridget and Alexa are friends. And a few years back Alexa came to Bridget with a problem. Josh was cheating on her. She didn't know how to make him stop and keep her family together."

Beckett just kind of stares at me in shock.

"Bridget saw me bury the journal when I was younger, so she knew where it was. She figured with the journal that Alexa would be able to force Josh to behave."

"Did it work?" He asks.

I shake my head. "From what I hear Josh is still a cheater, he just does so quietly now and apparently Alexa is fine enough with that as long as it means her children still have a father and she still has a husband."

Beckett's eyes stare out the front window. "That sounds like a horrible way to live."

I nod.

"Quinn, we don't have to do this." Beckett glances over at me. "We could all just go about our lives and leave this alone." But he doesn't sound convincing when he says it.

I pull the car into the neighborhood. "Can you really do that, Beckett?" I challenge. "I know you might want to, but I've seen how far you've gone for this journal. Can you truly get this close and just let it go?"

"No." He takes a deep breath. "I want to, for you, Quinn."

"I know you do." I smile softly.

"But..." His jaw ticks. "No, I can't just let it go."

"I know that too." I smile again but this one is weaker. "I'll still be here on the other side of whatever it is you have to do."

He grabs my free hand as I turn onto their street. "Thank you, Quinn."

I nod a little and pull towards their house, having gotten the address from Bridget. She said that Alexa should be home for the day after Christmas but apparently Josh is working down at the station. I can't believe the asshole became a cop. At least my sister is higher up on the food chain than he is.

When I put the car in park Beckett takes my face in his hands and presses a desperate kiss to it. He licks at my tongue as our mouths collide. I can feel his hands slip to my sides, clearly wanting to go lower, but stopping short.

"Thank you." He repeats as he pulls away from the kiss.

I nod. "Just... please don't lose yourself trying to avenge someone who's already gone." I press my forehead to his both of us breathless, "Lila wouldn't want that for you and I don't want that for you either."

"I'll try." And with that he gets out of the car.

Chapter Nineteen

Quinn

I follow Beckett up to the front door and he knocks on it hard. There are kids screaming inside, clearly audible even through the door. When the knock sounds another shout goes through the house. "Quiet!" Alexa comes to answer the door and when she pulls it open her eyes are already fixed in a glare.

Her blonde highlights are grown out half way down her face with a harsh line of demarcation. She has bags under her eyes and wrinkles across her face that make her look much older than her years. She turns back to glance at her children before stepping out onto the porch of their dingy gray house, closing the door behind herself.

"Quinn, Beckett, I haven't seen you both in years." She seems immediately suspicious both in her guarded stance, with her arms across her chest and her tight facial expression.

"How have you been?" I ask, trying to break some of the tension.

She glares at me. "You care now, city slut?"

Apparently this conversation would not be staying cordial like I had been hoping. Years of an untamed grudge will do that I suppose.

Beckett straightens his back so his height is towering over her even more than it was. "Don't talk to her like that." He growls. "She was trying to be polite, now you're going to have to deal with me."

Alexa takes a step back. "Why are you here, Beckett?"

"I want Lila's journal." He growls. "And you're going to give it to me, or I'm going to spend the next few hours ransacking your house until I find it while Quinn entertains your kids and you're locked in the basement."

She goes to grab her phone out of her pocket, likely to call her husband, but Beckett is faster and snatches it up from her hand. "You can't do that."

He tosses the phone at me. "Try me, Alexa." I catch it and tuck it into my purse. "I want the journal. I know you have it. Where is it?"

She shakes her head. "I don't know what you're talking about, psycho."

"Let's step inside." Beckett nods at the door, making it clear with his eyes that this is not a suggestion. "Wouldn't want your neighbors hearing us argue about your husband's extracurricular activities."

Alexa grits her teeth.

I swallow hard trying to remind myself that Beckett isn't like this. This is him trying to find something he's been looking for half his life, he's not this person to me.

She turns and heads back into the house. "Come in, assholes." She mutters. "No swearing around the kids."

Beckett and I follow in behind her and she leads us through the foyer into the kitchen. "Where are your kids?"

"Playroom upstairs." She answers. "They aren't a part of this." She rushes out, trying to make it clear that they are off limits.

"Understood." Beckett says.

Alexa takes a seat, just about collapsing down onto one of the chairs at her round kitchen table. "I knew when Bridget gave me that journal that it would be nothing but trouble." She runs a hand through her knotted hair and it gets caught.

"So you do have it?" I clarify.

Alexa nods. "Well... I did."

Beckett sits down across from her. "What is that supposed to mean?"

Alexa looks between the two of us before settling her gaze on me. "I never believed you at the time." She says, chewing on her lip. "I'm sorry about that."

I lean back against the counter. "It was a long time ago."

"Yet here you are at my front door looking for the journal like not a day has passed since." She huffs before turning her attention down and staring at the table. "I should have believed you. My life would have gone very differently had I believed you."

"I don't know how to respond to that."

Alexa shrugs. "Just know I'm sorry."

A moment passes through the room and the only sound is the kids still screaming upstairs, it's making me wonder if she should be checking on that, but she doesn't move.

Beckett's tone softens as he leans forwards towards her, "Alexa, where is the journal?"

"Gone." She whispers.

I just blink at her.

"What do you mean gone?" Beckett growls.

She backs away from him in her chair. "Josh found it." She answers. "For a couple years I was able to keep it hidden. I was able to use it against him and he stopped cheating... But then one day I came home and the house was torn apart. I had been hiding the journal in one of the floorboards under the bed, and he found it."

Beckett's fist slams down onto the table as his face creases in anger. "Fuck." He curses.

"When I got home the journal was burning in our fireplace along with the photo copies I had of it and my flash drives with the pictures of it." Alexa shakes her head. "I'm sorry, Beck–ett."

He kicks his chair back with a shout and starts pacing the floor of the kitchen. "No." He mutters. "No, I... it can't be gone." He growls.

Alexa and I both shrink back against his rage. "I'm so sorry, Beckett." Alexa apologizes again. "But I don't have it anymore."

"I-" He's about to speak again when the front door slams open.

"WHAT THE FUCK ARE YOU DOING HERE, BECKETT!?" Comes screaming from down the hallway, I immediately recognize the voice as Josh's.

"You set us up." Beckett growls at Alexa.

I fish her phone out of my purse and see a call still going, a call to Josh... he heard everything and he knew we were here. I hang up the phone. "She must have called him before she answered the door." I toss the phone onto the ground and smash it with my heel.

Josh comes barging into the kitchen, luckily by himself and not with a weapon like I was expecting. "What the fuck are you doing here?" He growls again, his dark brown eyes alight with fury. His short brown hair is shaggy and unkept. I can't help but notice he has the same bags under his eyes that Alexa does.

Beckett grabs my hand, pulling me behind him. "We were just leaving."

Josh puts a hand on Beckett's chest to stop him. He's not as tall as Beckett, but it's close. "You come into my house, harass my wife, and then you think you can just leave?"

Beckett drops my hand and chuckles darkly. "You don't want to touch me right now."

Josh shoves him backwards. "Why the fuck not, asshole?" He growls. "You forced your way into my house and it's mine and my wife's word against yours and Quinn's for what happens here today." He leans in. "Everyone knows Quinn is a fucking liar."

Before I can even process it, Beckett's fist is going through Josh's jaw and I hear a re-sounding crack echo through the space. Beckett shakes his hand out with a smile. "I've been wanting to do that for almost fifteen fucking years."

But it's at that moment that I notice some-one coming in the front door. "Police!" Some-one yells loudly.

A few officers come into the kitchen and see Josh with his jaw clearly now broken and Beckett standing menacingly over him. It doesn't take a genius to put two and two to-gether, but Josh makes it clear. "This asshole punched me in the fucking face."

No one bothers to try and discern anything else that happened. "Sir, hands behind your back." The first officer says.

Beckett's head kicks back realizing he was set up and does as the officer asks. "I'm sorry, Quinn." Beckett says as the officer cuffs him and starts to pull him out the door.

"You're a fucking asshole." I growl at Josh.

Josh just shrugs. "Get out of my house, Quinn. Before I have them arrest you for tres-passing."

I don't hesitate, following behind my boyfriend and the cops. "Trust me, I don't want to be here any longer than I fucking have to be." I just about run from the house and go hop in the cab of Beckett's truck.

There's a solid six squad cars lining the street and I can't help be feel like that's a little fucking excessive. The lights flash and I wish we would have stayed in the fucking living room so we could have seen them from the windows.

Beckett gets tossed rather roughly into the back of one of the cars while another officer starts walking with Josh outside as an ambu-lance shows up. Now that is fucking excessive. Josh heads to the ambulance and I watch from Beckett's truck as he gets checked out with a fucking smile on his face.

I pull my phone out of my purse and call Ashley.

She answers after a few rings, her cheerful voice coming through the speaker phone. "Hey, Quinn, how are–"

I cut her off. "Is Caleb there?" I rush out.

"Are those sirens?" She asks. "Quinn, are you okay?"

I shake my head, even though I know she can't see it. Tears start streaming down my face and I can't help but feel like this is my fucking fault. I brought him here. He was going to just let it go and I brought him into the viper's den. "Is Caleb there?" I ask again.

"Yeah." There is shuffling on the other side of the line before I hear, "Here he is."

"Quinn, what's going on?" Caleb asks.

"Beckett got arrested." I answer.

"Why am I not surprised?" Caleb sighs. "Don't tell me anything on the phone. I'll meet you at your parents' house. You can fill me in on what happened and then I'll meet Beckett at the station. If you're around him, tell him not to say anything."

"They already took him." I take a deep breath, trying to calm the fuck down. "Caleb, this is my fault, I–"

"No." He growls. "Don't say another damned word over the phone. Actually as a matter of fact I'm going to hang up. I'll meet you at your dad's house." And then the line goes dead.

I spent at least ten minutes crying in Beckett's truck before I got myself put together enough to drive over to my parents' house. I may or may not have spent most of my drive over crying too, but I was at least more put together than the erratic sobs from before. I don't love the thought that Josh probably fucking saw how upset I was but that's just what it is I guess.

I pull into the driveway of my parents' house and see Caleb and Ashley's minivan already there. I put Beck's truck in park and give myself another second to breathe before I actually get out. "I can do this. I can handle this." I tell myself as I climb out of the cab.

The door is opened the second I get to it and Caleb, wearing a damned suit, is on the other side. "Come into the kitchen, away from the kids."

I nod and follow him past Ash and their children who are all playing in the living room with different toys they got from Christmas. I see Adriane and my dad sitting at the counter, but not my sister.

He closes the kitchen door behind me, which almost never happens in this house. "Bridget went to the station to check on what's happening with Beckett." Caleb says, answering my question before I even asked it. "Now what happened?"

"It's a long story..." I say, chewing on my lip.

Caleb shakes his head. "I don't need that. I need the facts of what happened at the time Beckett got arrested. Did they read him his rights?"

I nod. "I think so."

"Did he stay quiet?" Caleb asks.

I nod again. "I think so?"

Caleb sighs. "Okay, now what happened that got him arrested?"

"He punched Josh in the face." I mutter, looking down at the floor sheepishly.

Caleb stifles a laugh. "Took him a damned decade. That man moves slow as fucking molasses. First with you and then with this. If he would have punched Josh at the fucking time no one would have blamed him."

I bristle a little.

Caleb ignores that though and continues to ask more questions. "Who all was there when it happened?"

"Beckett, Josh, Alexa, and me."

Caleb nods. "Did you say you saw the punch to anyone?"

I shake my head.

"Good, don't, because you didn't." Caleb grabs his briefcase off the kitchen counter. "I'm going down to the station. Stay here. I'll have him bailed out by the end of the night." And with that he leaves the kitchen, "Door open or closed?" And I realize after a second he's asking my dad.

"Closed." My dad says.

Caleb does as my dad asks and slides the door back into place. I swallow hard feeling the ominous tone running through the room. Before I can get a lecture about how I should stay away from Beckett, I turn and run after Caleb.

"I'm going with you!"

Caleb shakes his head. "It's better if I go alone."

"I don't care." I tell him. "I'm coming with."

My dad comes out of the kitchen, followed by Adriane, neither of them moving at any great speed. "Quinn, you need to stay here." His tone is stern and it reminds me of when I used to get scolded for doing something stupid as a child.

"No." I say plainly. "He's my boyfriend, and I want to help him so I'm going with Caleb."

My dad goes to argue again but Caleb cuts him off. "We aren't having this discussion in front of the kids. If Quinn wants to come with she can. She's an adult, she can make her own decisions. Even if I would strongly advise against it."

"Noted." I huff. "Can we go?"

Caleb opens the door and gestures through it. "After you."

I go to leave, but my dad grabs my arm. "Be careful, Quinn. I don't want the next phone call I get to be that you're arrested too. Don't let Beckett drag you down with him."

I shake him free and storm out of the house.

Caleb follows behind me. "We can drive separately. I'll wait for you when I get there and for the love of god, Quinn. Don't say anything about what happened. I don't care who asks you, I don't care what they say their intentions are. You say nothing. Don't lie either, just say nothing. Tell them to talk to your lawyer."

"I get it, Caleb." I climb into the driver's seat of Beckett's truck. "I'll keep my mouth shut." I promise as I close the door behind me.

He looks less than convinced, but he goes and gets in Ashley's minivan anyways, deciding not to argue with me further. Caleb pulls out of the driveway and I follow behind him. The police station is in the middle of town so it doesn't take too long to get there.

The entire drive over all I can do is think about Beckett. I shouldn't have brought him there. I should have just let him leave the journal alone like he wanted to. This is my fault.

That guilt sits heavier and heavier in my stomach the closer we get to the police station. If I thought I owed him one before I owe him a lot more now.

The old two story building is long enough to cut off several cross streets. The dark gray brick is covered in snow and ice with salt tossed haphazardly to try and melt it all. Its foreboding nature makes it loom high on the horizon in the dark winter sky as I pull into the parking lot.

I don't want to go in.

I really don't know why I came with, I just... didn't want to get a lecture. I think I might want to see my boyfriend in a cell less. This was a bad idea. I clearly didn't think this all the way through. I haven't been thinking a lot of things through lately.

I stare at the front doors and after a second there is a knock on the window.

"Shake the lead out, Quinn!" Caleb calls from the other side. "Either come in or don't but I need to go make sure they are following due process."

"I'm coming." I open the door and climb out of the truck. "Okay... Okay. I can do this." I mutter to myself, but I'm sure Caleb heard it.

"Great pep talk, but what you need to do is nothing. Just shut up and stand there." Caleb says sternly.

"I got it." I grumble, following behind him into the police station. The glass doors feel cold in my ungloved hands and I feel very under-dressed only realizing now that I'm still in my plaid pajama pants and Beckett's hoodie. At least I have my peacoat covering the hoodie, but the pants I'm stuck with.

The station is a mass of desks sprawled out in the wide, blue gray room with that kind of dense carpeting that is hard underfoot. Caleb approaches the receptionist and asks some questions in a hushed tone that I don't quite make out over the pounding in my ears.

I don't see Beckett but there are a few hallways leading off in different directions and a handful of doors lining the room so he could still be here.

The receptionist picks up his phone and calls someone on it, waving us off. "You can take a seat, Officer Thompson will be with you in a few minutes, he's chatting with someone about this case already, but he can see you in a moment."

"I'm his lawyer." Caleb argues. "I need to see my client now."

The receptionist shakes his head. "Mr. Campbell already has a lawyer."

"Who?" I ask.

"I can't answer that question." The receptionist says, "But if you wait a few moments you can talk with the officer running the case and Mr. Campbell's lawyer should be out shortly."

"Caleb?" I look to him like he would magically fix all of this.

He just goes to sit down. "If he already has a lawyer, I can't do anything." Caleb says. "We could leave now, but if you want to see him, I'll wait here with you."

I glare at the receptionist and turn in a huff to sit down next to Caleb. "Whatever."

Chapter Twenty

Quinn

I find myself falling asleep in the chair before Beckett even gets out. So much for a few minutes. Damned receptionist. Everyone just lets me sleep though, apparently I seem like I need it.

After I don't know how long, I feel someone gently start to shake me awake. "Quinn." When I recognize the voice to be Beckett's I just about jump out of my seat.

My eyes shoot open and I see him crouched in front of me. I throw myself at him, almost tackling him to the ground in a hug. "I'm so fucking sorry."

"It's not your fault, Quinn." He promises immediately. "There was just a mix up." Beckett smirks. "Right, Mr. Connors?"

I glance up to see a tall man in his thirties wearing a suit and tie. "Exactly." He smiles. "Now, let's get the hell out of here."

"Gladly." Beckett pulls me to my feet. He guides me from the police station. "Wait in the truck, I'll explain what happened in a minute."

I nod and dart for the passenger seat, wanting to get as far away from the building that took my boyfriend as physically possible. I see Beckett discuss a few more things with Connors before giving him a hug and turning towards me.

I shrink in my seat as he climbs into the truck. "What happened?"

Beckett closes the door behind him. He starts to pull out of the parking spot, sighing heavily as he does. "I didn't break Josh's jaw." He says it like he's almost disappointed. "And since there were no strong witnesses and I'm an upstanding citizen, Jacob convinced the arresting officer that it was in their best interest to just drop the charges."

"And they just did?" I ask confused.

"Jacob is the old fire chief's son. Turns out the old fire chief and the current police chief are drinking buddies. And Jacob just so happens to represent the arresting officer's dealer." Beckett sighs. "Everyone knows everyone in this town."

"That was a large part of why I left." I mutter softly.

"But between the lack of a strong case and the soft threat that the chief might learn about the arresting officer's coke problem. The charges got dropped." Beckett's jaw ticks. "I don't love that being the reason I got out but it's better than sitting in jail for however long."

"I'm so fucking sorry."

Beckett glances over at me as he drives us to where I don't know. "You don't have to be sorry, Quinn."

"I shouldn't have pushed you to go after the journal again." I play with my thumbs in my hands. "You said you wanted to let it go. I should have just let you."

Beckett huffs a laugh.

"What?" I furrow my brow.

"Quinn, I was never going to let it go."

"What do you mean?" I blink at him.

He keeps his eyes on the road for a moment, not answering my question. "You have a tell, you know. When you lie."

I don't immediately make the connection.

"You wrinkle your nose." He chuckles. "It's actually kind of cute. I've never been able to figure out if I have a tell." Another breath passes through the car. "Quinn, I was never going to just move on. I didn't know what my next steps were, but I knew I would keep going after the journal. And now that it's gone..."

I've gathered by now he's driving back toward his place, which is almost a relief because it means he's not taking me back home. I was a little scared he was going to break up with me after all of this.

"I know what I have to do." He says with a conviction that reminds me of the night he set the bookstore on fire. A conviction that scares me to my bones.

I shake my head. "I don't think I want to know."

Beckett nods. "You don't." He agrees. "But can I ask you something?"

"What is it?" I shift in my seat.

"What was in the journal?"

I freeze, a chill running down my spine even in the warmth of the truck. I shake my head. "No... No, I'm not answering that question."

"Quinn." He pleads softly, glancing over at me. "Please, I've spent a decade searching for it. You read it, I know you did that was why you went after it when the police had it."

I chew on my lip, but don't respond.

Apparently his patience ran thin because he growls, "What was in the journal, Quinn?" Making it clear that this time, it's not a question, it's a demand.

"No." I push back.

"No?" He sneers. "Why?"

"Because there are some things that some people aren't meant to know." I cross my arms over my chest, falling back into my convictions. I never thought he should have the journal, but I let myself get blinded by how much I like him. By the feeling that I owed him for upending his life for me. "I won't tell you."

As if he could hear my thoughts he pulls at my guilt, "Quinn, I'm moving to New York for you–"

"I didn't ask you to do that!" I just about scream back at him. I take a breath trying to steady myself. "You don't have to move to New York for me. That was your choice. I was perfectly okay with this being some fun fling we had one winter."

His face tightens. Beckett stares out at the road, leaving my words hanging out in the air, but I notice he's changed the direction of the truck, and now we are driving back towards my parents'.

I fight the urge to start crying. I don't want him to see me like that. I don't want him to know how much this is affecting me. I said I was fine with us being a fling and I have to mean it or I'm just going to be letting my heart get broken by someone who I'm not even sure deserves a piece of it.

I wrap my arms around myself, trying to put my head on straight but struggling every time I think about how I'm *still* wearing this man's fucking hoodie. I want to take it off but I need something to wear to get to my room besides just my coat.

Beckett pulls the truck into the driveway and looks at me like he's about to say something, but I don't want to know what it is.

I climb out of the truck and slam the car door hard behind me. I don't look at him, but I know he's watching me as I climb up the steps to the porch and make my way inside the house.

"Quinn." Adriane's voice peaks up like she's surprised. "What are you doing back? Caleb said you were with Beckett."

I shoulder my coat off and hang it up by the door before taking off my boots too. Tears stream softly down my face but I fight the urge to all out sob until I'm alone.

"Quinn?" Adriane calls again, pushing up off the couch and coming over to check on me.

I ignore her and try not to run as I head down the hall and up the stairs away from everyone. I get up to my room and collapse onto the bed, the second I do I'm sobbing into the pillow, cursing his fucking name and wishing that things would have gone differently.

I should have never opened up to him. I should have never had sex with him. I knew it was a mistake. I just wanted to feel reckless, impulsive. Well this is what impulsive gets you, a broken heart and a jackass who I want nothing more than to go running after right now.

Maybe I should just catch a flight to New York tonight. I would feel better drunk at some bar in Manhattan with Madison that I will here crying in my room. Madison would get me royally wasted and I could find some new jackass to hook up with.

Fuck Beckett.

I'm maybe in my room for a minute before there is a knock at the door. I don't answer, preferring to wallow alone, but the door opens anyways.

"I would have been here sooner, but with the baby, I don't move around as well as I used to." Adriane chuckles softly, coming to sit down on the bed. "I will be so happy when I finally give birth."

I glance at her and try not to glare.

"Right, this isn't about that." Adriane shifts a little on the bed. "What happened, Quinn?"

I take a few deep breaths trying to calm myself down so I can actually think. So I can actually try and explain literally anything. I don't know if Adriane is really the person I want to be talking to. I want to call Madison, but I don't know where my phone is right now and at least Adriane is someone.

"Beckett said he was going to move to New York." I sniffle.

"Isn't that a good thing?" She asks, brushing some of her blonde hair out of her face. "If he moves you can see him more."

"It's too much." I push up from my stomach and join Adriane sitting back against the headboard. "The relationship doesn't have anything to stand on and him packing up his life to move to New York for me? I can't ask him to do that. I could never owe him that much."

"Did you ask him to?"

"No." I whisper. "But he already held it against me. He already used it like a weapon, like something I need to pay him back for. And I don't want to have to repay that debt."

Adriane nods, "You know, when Bridget and I started talking about getting pregnant, we had to figure out who would carry the baby."

I furrow my brow. "What does this have to do with anything?"

"Your whole family, you have no patience." She sighs and I bristle. "Just let me finish my story."

"Go on." I gesture with a wave.

"Bridget didn't want to be the one to carry the baby. She knew about your mother's close calls when you two were born and the mis-carriages that run in your family." Her voice is gentle and full of sorrow. "So Bridget was scared to risk her own life to try and bring us a baby."

"Me?" Adriane smiles and brings a hand to her stomach. "I wasn't scared. I was more than willing to put myself at risk to bring me and Bridge the family we always dreamed of. And Bridget, she said she wasn't sure she could ever owe me that. She wasn't sure she would ever be able to repay that kind of debt to me. And you know what I said?"

I shake my head.

"I told her there was no debt. There was nothing she owes me or could ever owe me because she and I are a team. We are two parts of one whole. If Beckett truly cares about you, if he truly wants to move to New York for you. Then there is no debt, Quinn. Because you don't keep score with people you love." Adriane takes my hand and squeezes it softly.

"Besides, if you were keeping score, he owes you for burning down your parents' bookstore." Adriane chuckles.

My eyes go wide. "How did you know?"

She shrugs. "I kept a hidden camera behind the counter. I checked the footage the next day but since you didn't report him I just left it alone. I figured you had your reasons."

"Thank you, Adriane."

She nods. "Beckett is cute, I get letting your pussy call the shots. I know I might be married and a lesbian but I have eyes."

I chuckle and wipe away the rest of my tears with his hoodie sleeve. "I should text him shouldn't I?"

"Do you want to text him, Quinn?"

I pat down my pants and find my phone in my pocket. "Yeah...I may have overreacted just a little bit. I think I owe him at least a text."

"Do what you think is right." She smiles softly, before pushing up off the bed. "I'm going to attempt my descent down stair mountain. Wish me luck." She salutes with a laugh and I salute back. Then Adriane leaves me with her words hanging in the air around me.

I stare down at my phone like I'm waiting for it to fucking bite me. I don't know if texting him is the right thing to do, but I want to talk to him. I don't like the way things were left between us, maybe I could just tell him that.

Me: I don't want to leave things like that.

And for a second I debate not hitting send, I debate not saying anything. My finger hovers over the button and I almost don't press down... but then I do, and my message is left out there floating in the ether.

Chapter Twenty One

Beckett

"Shake the lead out, chief!" Albert calls to me as I stare at the ablaze cabin with a toothy smile spread across my face. At least no one is really looking at me.

I've always been fascinated by fire, it's a large part of why I got into this job, and I've never seen a fire of this magnitude before. It's magnificent. This is no ordinary kitchen fire. This is a masterpiece. This was intentional.

Two pedestrians stand outside the burning building, their clothes reeking of smoke when I walk past them, but I've set enough bonfires to recognize the smell of something else too, lighter fluid.

The man is tall, taller than me even which is surprising cause it's rare I met someone *taller than me. Every inch of exposed skin other than his face is covered in tattoos, even partially his neck. His Henley hangs tight on his body as he holds his partner against him.*

The woman leans her head back into him, her blonde hair swaying in the breeze. While his face is severe, hers is soft, but she doesn't seem even slightly alarmed by the situation unfolding around her. Her hazel eyes just drifting over the fire lightly like this is any other Tuesday.

"Albert!" I call as he starts pulling the hose out of the truck. "Has anyone talked to the civilians yet?"

He laughs. "That's your job now, chief."

Right. This is a newer appointment. I haven't been chief for even a year at this point and this is the first major fire we've seen in a decade. I need to focus.

I walk over to the couple, standing there snuggling like they aren't watching a building burn down and nod. "I'm chief Campbell."

"Got a first name?" The man asks gently.

"Beckett, Beck." I tell him.

He reaches out his hand. "Danny Blakely."

I shake his hand back and his partner extends her hand next.

"Izzy Blakely." She smiles.

I shake her hand too before she seems to lose herself back into her husband. She plays with her yellow and pink sundress straps and when she does he kisses her cheek.

"Do you know if there is anyone else inside the building?"

Mr. Blakely sighs softly like he's bored. "Shouldn't be. This was a weekend get away for just the two of us." He runs his fingers over his wife's side. Something about his answer feels ominous.

"Well I'm sorry to see your weekend plans got ruined." I apologize half heartedly. I hear my team working to start putting out the fire and glance behind me with eyes full of envy. Why did I ever agree to this boring fucking job?

"You want to be with them." The man who I'm not convinced is actually Danny Blakely says. Everything about him feels like he's hiding something.

I pull my attention back to the conversation. "I'm fine." I assure him.

He tilts his head to the side. "So nothing is bothering you?" He leans into me. "Not even your sister's disappearance?"

My eyes go wide. "I don't... Who are you?"

"A friend." He smiles. "One who needs a favor."

I scoff. "What kind of favor?"

He pulls out his phone and his fingers fly across the keyboard. "I need that house to be rubble." He keeps his tone and face light despite his words. "Maybe the water on the hose stops working. Maybe the fire starts again. But I need it burned to ash."

I shake my head. "What the fuck makes you think I will help you with that? My job is to put fires out, not keep them going."

"Because, pyro." He smirks as I bristle at him. "I've done the leg work for you to find that journal you've been searching for."

I narrow my eyes. "Who are you actually?"

He seems to consider answering my question, but his wife beats him to the punch. "Liam, stop toying with him. He has a job to do... or not do, right, Beck?"

I glance back over my shoulder again. "Do you actually know what happened to Lila's journal?"

Liam shrugs. "I know a lot of things. And I like to share information with my friends." He leans in. "Are you a friend, Beck?"

For a second I consider the moral and ethical implications of what I'm being asked to do. But then the practical ones. "The suits have cameras."

Liam shakes his head. "Disabled."

"I..."

The woman leans forward. "I'm Riley." She smiles. "Look, I get the hesitation, but it's no different than the controlled burns that you did for practice back when you were in school. It's just that we started this one instead."

"I don't like this." I mutter.

Liam shrugs. "You don't have to. A lot of people do things they don't like. Trust me, my job isn't all handjobs and roses either."

"I'm almost positive that's not the saying." Riley chuckles.

Liam waves her off. "I'll deal with you later." He turns his attention back to me. "But if you're going to do anything you need to do it now before they actually manage to get the fire out." He smiles again that one that feels like I'm making a deal with the devil. "Do it for Lila."

I growl but I turn around and pull a switchblade out of my pocket. I walk up to one of the hoses, checking to make sure no one is around. Then I stand to the side and slice it clean through. I move away from it quickly and find my way back towards Liam and Riley, pretending that I never left their side to begin with.

The hose starts to squirt water out of the leak instead of the end and the spray gets weak. The person manning it looks confused before glancing back and seeing the ground starting to flood as the hose spills out water.

"What can you tell me about the journal?" I ask him.

He shakes his head. "Not today. Today you worry about holding up your end of the deal, tomorrow we can talk about what you want."

"No." I push.

"No?" He questions softly, but his voice has a harsh quality to if that makes me uncomfortable.

"I want to know where the journal is now." I tell him. "I don't know who you are and what you're asking me to do could get me arrested and/or fired so no. If you tell me where the journal is..." I take a deep breath, "Then I'll help you."

Liam smirks.

"I told you." Riley mutters.

"Fine." Liam concedes. "Quinn O'Brady was the last person I was able to find who had it. As far as I can tell she stole it from the police and hid it, but I don't know where."

The name hits me like a punch in the fucking gut. I had a crush on Quinn for years and honestly a part of me never got over that. But that's a problem for another day.

"Now go make sure that cabin is destroyed." Liam growls. "You don't want to see how I handle when people break deals with me."

I nod. By the end of the night the cabin is rubble and I have the phone number of a very dangerous man sitting in the pocket of my turnout gear.

It's been a day since I got that text message from Quinn and I know I should text her back, but I just... I haven't felt ready. I know leaving her on read isn't helping anything. I don't know what she's thinking right now, but I'm still planning on moving to New York. I'm done with this town; with or without her I'm leaving.

If for no other reason than soon enough I'm going to have to. I've decided since Josh isn't going to be brought to justice any other way that it's time to take matters into my own hands. But the only problem is, I've never killed anyone before. I don't really know where to start.

I can't very well just google it because even hidden browsers can be traced back to you. But I do know someone who I think might be able to help me.

The phone rings and I wait on baited breath.

"Hello." A soft female voice lilts through the phone.

"I'm looking for Liam." I know this run around. I've called him a few times and every time his wife answers the phone first.

"I'm sorry. Who is this?" She feigns soft confusion, even though I'm more than positive that Liam has the best caller ID known to fucking mankind. I don't really know exactly what he does, but I've ascertained that calling him extremely tech savvy would be an understatement.

"Beckett." I grumble, I know it's not her fault but the run around is exhausting. "I have some business questions for him."

There is a pause on the other end of the line and then muted silence before the call ends. A second later there is another call from an unknown number. I answer it immediately.

"What do you want?" Liam huffs, not sounding angry but rather bored.

I think about what the fuck to ask for a second before finally settling on, "How secure is this line? Can anyone trace this call or find it later?"

"Nothing is truly ever fully hidden, but this is about as secure as you're going to get without being in person." Liam answers. "Why?"

I take a deep breath. "The journal is gone."

"What do you want to do about that?"

"I want to get rid of something else." I say, trying to make my point clear without speaking my actual intentions.

There is a pause on the other end of the line. "How much true crime do you watch?" He chuckles.

"Next to none." I reply.

"Then you're screwed." Liam says.

"I was wondering if I could call in a favor from a friend." I say carefully, knowing full well I'm about to put myself in a tough position. Owing Liam another favor, especially an open ended one seems dangerous, but I'm desperate. "We are friends. Aren't we?"

Liam laughs. "I suppose we are." There is a pause. "How's packing going? Got room for two in your house?"

"You're coming here?" I ask confused.

"You'd get yourself arrested again if you did anything on your own." Liam states plainly. "I can't talk about what you need to do on the phone and I did win a private jet from a friend earlier this year that hasn't gotten nearly enough use. So yeah, Riley and I will be there in a few hours."

I shake my head. "My entire place is in boxes."

His shrug is audible. "Then buy some blow up mattresses." The line goes dead.

Chapter Twenty Two

Quinn

I walk down stairs into the kitchen, it's been over a day with no word from Beckett and I'm starting to think he won't be calling or texting me back ever again. My dad sits at the kitchen counter alone with a cup of coffee and his tablet looking at the news.

As I walk to make myself a cup of coffee my mind immediately starts to drift to Christmas morning waking up with Beckett. I start thinking about us sitting in the kitchen making plans together not even that long ago.

I sniffle softly, pouring the creamer and then the coffee into the cup.

"He's not worth it, Quinn." My father's tone is soft. "He's not worth your tears. Any man who is worth your time will treat you right and if he is making you feel like this... He's not treating you right."

"I-" I get cut off by the sound of my phone ringing in my pocket. I pull it free and see unknown scrawled across the top. I answer annoyed, "Beckett, I thought I told you to call from your actual number."

"It's not Beckett." A man replies. I don't immediately recognize his voice but it has a familiarity to it.

I glance up from my coffee to my dad. "I have to take this." I tell him, clearing up the last of my sniffles, taking my coffee, and beelining for the front door. "Who is this?" I mutter softly into the phone as I shoulder on my jacket over my sweater.

I pull on my boots waiting for the answer but he just replies, "Almost outside yet?"

My hand was on the door handle, but hesitation courses through me at his words. "Why?" I ask, cautiously.

"Because your ride is here." His smirk audible through the phone and that's when it hits me. I do know this man's voice. One of my clients under the pen name Maddie Luna, she got married this year. I've only met her husband a handful of times at different events I went to with Madison, but Riley I know fair-ly well. What the fuck was her husband's name?

He hangs up the phone and I pocket it.

I pull open the door handle to see Beckett's truck sitting in the driveway. Quickly, I down the rest of my coffee and abandon the mug on the porch, I can pick it back up later. I'm fairly relieved when I get to the truck and I see Beckett in the driver's seat, but I'm more than a little confused at who's sitting beside him.

Beckett rolls his window down. "Get in, fire-bug." He purrs.

Riley's husband laughs in the passenger seat. "Cute. Riley just calls me stronzo." I recognize the word both from hearing Riley mutter it at him during video chats and from my summer in Italy a few years back.

"Why are you here?" I ask Beckett, before turning my attention to Riley and... I'll re-member in a minute here, "Why are all of you here?"

"Get in, Quinn." Her husband smirks, nod-ding at the backseat. His words are soft and friendly, but something about his eyes make it clear it's a demand.

So stupidly, I open up the door and climb into the back seat beside Riley. "Hi." I smile at her.

She goes in for a hug and so that I'm not being rude I do reciprocate. "It's so good to see you!" She smiles. "Your firm told me you were on vacation for the holidays and have been holding all my messages." She pouts a little before gesturing to her husband. "You remember Liam."

Oh thank god, I so was not going to remember that. "Hi." I mutter again, nodding at him.

"Quinn." Liam smiles politely.

Beckett starts to back the truck down the driveway.

I swallow, something about Riley's husband has always made me... uneasy. I know she loves him, but... Her and I have known each other for years, and she went off the grid for just a bit too long when she met him. I was more than a little worried about her at the time. "Where are we going?"

Beckett and Liam look between each other. "Right now, back to my place." Beckett answers. "We need to talk somewhere that as Liam puts it, is more secure than a truck."

The car ride back is tense for a short while before Riley starts chatting with me about her books. I quickly lose myself in that conversation. I had been missing work and just Madison's book hadn't been enough for me. Being able to pretend like everything was fine for a moment and hearing that Riley was planning on having me edit something else was a relief. If I was about to get killed Riley wouldn't be trying to book me for January.

We pull up to Beckett's place and all climb out of the car. I follow the crowd inside playing with my phone in my pocket. My eyes dart around outside Beckett's house trying to figure out what the hell I'm doing here.

I was pretty sure that Beckett and I broke up and I had absolutely no idea he knew Riley and Liam. Them being here feels more than a little alarming especially with how scary Riley's husband is.

We get inside the house and Beckett locks the door behind us.

"Your phone." Liam says, holding a hand out.

I cautiously pull it out of my pocket and pass it over. "I don't like this."

Liam shrugs. "If we were going to kill you, you'd already be dead." And that is absolutely not a fucking comfort, rather just a reminder how psycho this man is. And apparently he and Beckett are friends.

He sets the phone down on the entry table before pulling out his own and setting it down too. Riley does the same and so does Beckett. Then Beckett takes my hand and drags me towards his bedroom.

I follow numbly, the anxiety making the blood pound loudly in my ears. "Beckett." I whimper out softly.

"We just need to talk somewhere private." He promises softly. Everyone follows into the room and Liam closes the door.

"Riley, maybe you should explain this." Liam offers.

She glares at her husband. "Oh yeah, make me tell her. Thanks."

"I'll reward you later." He promises darkly.

Riley chews on her lip for a second before walking over to me, taking my hands, and coming to sit down with me on the bed. She brushes some of her honey blonde hair away from her face as she starts to speak. "Josh can't continue to live."

My eyes go wide.

"And Beckett, as much as he may want to, is already on the police's radar." Riley says simply. "So he can't be anywhere near the house when this happens."

"When what happens?" I question.

"You're going to burn it down." Liam says as if it's that fucking simple and I'm just going to go along with that.

I blink at him. "I'm going to what?"

Riley takes back over then. "Beckett will make sure the house doesn't go out, but as for actually burning it down... someone needs to be inside to start the fire."

"What... what about Alexa and the kids?"

Liam smirks, seeming rather proud of himself. "Someone tipped Alexa off to that Josh has a mistress a few towns over... again. So this morning Alexa and the kids went to her mom's in Maine for a few days."

"Well can't that *someone* burn the house down instead of me?" I want to glare at him but I'm a little too scared to so I kinda just keep my eyes on Beckett.

"That someone doesn't like to do leg work unless they have to." Liam says. "And besides this isn't my fight. You're lucky I'm going to be doing as much as I am already."

"Which is what exactly?" I grumble.

Liam pauses and the room goes silent. "First of all, I'm going to ignore your tone because my wife particularly likes you and I don't want you to quit. She spent far too long searching for a good editor the first time."

I swallow.

"I'm going to take care of the cameras, his phone, and anything else electronically that could cause you to get caught." Liam answers. "And you are going to fix your attitude or someone is going to fix it for you."

I look to Beckett who's expression is just as hard as Liam's. I try glancing at Riley as my next route to appeal and she just smiles at me softly. Liam's green eyes glare at me and I can feel them even without looking.

Taking a deep breath, I shake my head. "I don't want to do this." I tell them. "I don't want to kill someone and I don't want to risk the jail time either." I say to the room, looking down at my feet.

"There's not going to be any jail time." Riley says simply. "Liam knows what he's doing and he's not going to let you walk in unprepared." Riley takes my hands again. "I promise you my husband will keep you safe."

Beckett comes and kneels down next to me. "Quinn." He pleads softly, "Are you really comfortable with Lila's killer having everything he wants? He left Lila behind in those woods and built himself the life of his dreams on her bones."

I look up at him.

"He doesn't deserve the life he has." Beckett states clearly. "He doesn't deserve to live at all. And someone needs to be the one to fix that." He reaches up and brushes some of my auburn hair away from my face. "The police are already going to pin me as the number one suspect unless my alibi is air fucking tight. But someone needs to bring justice for Lila."

Tears run softly down my face as I watch his eyes start to water. "Lila deserves more than she got." Beckett whispers. "You were her best friend. I know you care about her just as much as I do. Please, Quinn."

I look between the three of them again, debating if this is truly something I could do let alone something I want to do. I debate the morals, whether killing him makes me the same as him or does it make me a bringer of justice and come up with no answers. And in the end there is one piece of logic that sticks out to me.

This is one hell of a thing for Beckett to owe me. This is bigger than moving to New York. This is bigger than Adriane having a baby. This is taking a life. And if Beck owes me that... I would feel a hell of a lot better about him moving to New York for me.

"Okay." I mutter. "I'll do it."

"Thank you." Beck takes my face in his hands and kisses me desperately. "Thank you, Quinn." He mutters against my lips as his kisses start to deepen. His hands slide to my coat and start pulling it down my body.

"Oh." Riley giggles.

Out of the corner of my eyes I see Liam grab her hand. "Let's go break the blow up mattress in the living room." He purrs as he drags his wife out of the bedroom, closing the door behind them.

My attention refocuses on Beck, who's still slowly undressing me. He gets the coat the rest of the way off and I reach down to the bottom of his t-shirt to start pulling it over his head. He pulls away from our kiss only long enough to get the shirt off and then he's immediately back to kissing me.

The rest of the clothes come off in a fury of lips and moans and hands flying every which way. Quicker than I was anticipating I find myself naked with Beck guiding me backwards down onto the bed.

His eyes lick over me, thirsty and full of lust. "Don't move." Beck orders, turning around to search for something in one of the dresser drawers behind him.

I lay on my back, still panting from our kiss, staring at his ceiling and trying to get my bearings. I feel so out of it, I feel so insane. Beck makes me feel insane, but in the best possible way. I don't lose myself to my thoughts long because I feel Beck roughly grab my arm a second later.

I instinctively try and pull back as he latches a handcuff around my wrist. I gasp, staring at him with wide eyes as he pulls me up from where I'm laying.

"Remember these." He purrs, bringing me to my knees in front of him and handcuffing the other wrist so they are behind my back.

I nod. "Yes." I whisper.

Beck smiles. "I want to thank you." He purrs as he twists my body so I'm facing the bed. "I want to show you just how grateful I am for what you're about to do for me." He pushes my chest down so I'm kneeling, bent over the side of the mattress.

I let out a huff of air and a whimper as I hit the mattress, adrenaline coursing through my veins. I turn my head to the side as much as I can to look up at him, but it's hard with his hand pinning my back down.

"Doesn't that sound nice, firebug?" He purrs as he moves to lay down on his back between my legs. "Sit on my face like a good slut."

I use my chest to push myself off the bed and slowly lower myself onto his face. I try to hover gently over him, but then he grabs my hips and pulls me down hard.

"I said to fucking sit, Quinn." Beck growls into my pussy lips. He licks up and down my slit a few times before coming to my center and sucking on the bundle of nerves there. I wouldn't be sure he was even breathing except for the fact that he keeps going beyond what would be possible if he wasn't.

Beck flicks his tongue over my clit back and forth as his hands grip roughly into my trembling thighs. I'm shaking, I know I'm shaking, but I can't fucking stop.

I have no way of measuring how much time is passing because all I can do is feel. Feel the pleasure he is eliciting between my legs. I'm soaking his face, my pussy is dripping fucking wet and I'm positive that when he finally does come up, his lips will taste of me. The thought of it making me want to kiss him more.

His devotion to satisfying me is irreverent like he's worshiping my pussy, like he'd forsake everything and anything fucking else if it meant that I would be pleased. He keeps licking and sucking and pinning me fucking down on to him so he has the angle he wants.

I feel myself getting closer the longer he keeps going. My head kicks back in a moan and when it does his tongue gets more feverish which I hadn't really thought even possible.

"Beck." I moan, grinding my hips trying to get myself to topple over the edge knowing I'm moments away from doing so. He keeps going and within seconds, I'm screaming out my orgasm. "Oh fuck!" I cry out toppling forward without my hands to catch me since they are still trapped behind my back.

It's in that moment I remember there are people in the other room who can probably fucking hear that I just finished. Then Riley lets out a scream followed by a very loud moan that almost feels like it was intentionally to compete with how loud I just was.

Beck and I ignore that as he lifts me up with his hands and moves me off of him. His cock is fully erected and I stare at him with hungry eyes wanting to feel him between my legs.

"Please..." I whimper as he sits upright. "Fuck me, Beck, please."

He smirks. "Gladly." Beck grabs the hand-cuffs and uses them to pin me back down to the bed. He positions himself between my legs behind me and I feel his cock rub over my slit. "You're fucking soaked, bug." He purrs.

I nod feverishly. "For you, always."

He grunts with desire as he pushes himself inside of me. I let out a guttural groan in return. "You're such a good fucking girl." His hips thrust into me roughly. "God, your pussy feels like damned heaven."

Beck starts to thrust into me and my eyes roll back. He holds the handcuffs by the chain using them to make me hover above the bed slightly. The tension is making my wrists sore but I almost don't care in that moment. All I care about is getting fucked hard enough that I'm screaming into this mattress.

"Harder." I moan.

He pushes me down onto the bed. "Harder?" He questions. "Can you handle harder, Quinn?"

I nod again. "Yes."

Beck chuckles darkly. He starts to move faster, going in deeper with each thrust. His movements are rough and full. He grunts with each thrust and I moan loudly in turn. He takes the encouragement and keeps going harder.

My body starts losing itself to the movements as my brain clouds over with bliss. My head is tilted to the side, my body keeps getting slammed into the mattress and it's true fucking euphoria, especially considering how sensitive I am in this moment. Every nerve ending feels like its on fire after my orgasm.

I want to do the same to him. I want him to finish between my legs and then I want to keep stimulating him so he feels the same pleasure pain high that I'm experiencing right now. "Fuck!" I scream, completely lost to the way he's making me feel.

Beck rolls his hips so that he's hitting a spot inside of me that has my eyes just about falling out of my head. I close them trying to keep myself semi put together, but not really succeeding.

"Quinn." He groans.

"Beck." I moan right back.

He moans my name again and I do the same. "You're everything I've ever fucking wanted." He purrs. "You're everything I've ever fucking imagined."

I have no idea how the fuck to respond to that. It feels like he's alluding to something more than what he said, but I don't know if we are ready for that yet. I mean... maybe? He did ask me to kill someone for him. And I fucking said yes. If that's not love...

Beck smacks my ass hard. "Focus, Quinn." He growls. "I can see you getting distracted. Lose yourself in me, firebug. Don't think. Just feel."

Don't think. Just feel.

Just *feel*.

He smacks my ass again and I let out a shriek at just how hard it is. His cock is rock fucking hard between my legs and I squeeze myself around him. I can still feel the handcuffs that are tight on my wrists. My tits are smashed up against his soft cotton sheets.

I roll myself back onto him and he pulls me down in tandem so our movements work together. "Yes." I moan.

"Good girl." He purrs. "Focus on me." He gives a few more thrusts before saying, "Quinn, I'm so fucking close. Tell me you want me to cum in you."

Warmth floods through me and I nod feverishly. "Yes, please. Finish in me, fuck, please finish in me, Beck." I keep begging and begging and a second later I feel him push fully into me.

Beck grunts loudly and I feel his cock twitching inside of me. The second he pulls out I feel the hot sticky liquid dribbling down my thighs and clench them shut. He pulls me upright by the handcuffs and turns me to kiss him. He tastes like my pussy just like I was expecting and I moan around the sweetness.

"I want to suck your cock." I breathe out.

He smirks. "Is that so?" Beck moves to sit down on the edge of the bed. He spreads his legs and I position myself between them. "Go ahead, firebug." He purrs.

I dip my head between his legs and start to bob myself up and down on his cock. After a second I feel his hands start to fist in my hair and I moan. I push myself as far down onto his length as I can get, but he's fucking huge. I go to lift my head back up, but Beck uses his grip on my hair to hold me there for a second. I struggle and he groans as he rolls his hips so his cock is rubbing up against the roof of my mouth and the back of my throat.

He's smiling as he pulls my lips back and starts using my hair like handles to fuck my face. He's still fucking hard even after he came. He rubs his head against the roof of my mouth and groans. I make a mental note to remember that for when I give him head in the future.

After a few more minutes he pulls all the way out. "Your mouth is divine." He tilts my head up and presses a kiss to my lips. "Now let's get you out of those handcuffs."

Chapter Twenty Three

Quinn

I can't believe I'm doing this. This is such a bad fucking idea and I could get myself fucking arrested. I should turn back. I should go back home and pretend none of this ever happened. But then Liam is stopping the van and I realize that's definitely not a fucking option.

"You'll be fine." He promises.

I bristle a little. "Who said I thought I wouldn't be?" I lie through my fucking teeth.

Liam chuckles. "Beck is right, your nose does crinkle when you lie."

My black gloved hands shoot up to my face and I cover my nose. "He's such a fucking asshole." I mutter.

"I can hear you." Beck smirks through the earpiece I'm wearing. This is all way more thought out and high tech than I was fucking expecting. This is a calculated execution and thinking about how it was planned on a moment's notice is more than a little scary.

"You'll be fine." Liam repeats. "I'll be in the van a few streets over. When you're done just run over here and we'll go."

I swallow hard, but I nod, grabbing the back-pack from the back of the van and holding it on my lap. "How do you turn these things off?" I ask Liam.

"The coms?" He asks. "You don't." He pulls his laptop off the dash and types a few things before asking. "Why?"

"Are they off?" I ask him.

He nods.

"I don't know if I can do this."

Liam sighs, but not like he's disappointed, more like he's understanding, or maybe reminiscing? "The first one is always the hardest." He looks out the window like he's lost in thought. "Grappling with how you feel about the loss of life that you caused, it kept me up more than a few nights."

I chew on my lip.

"You can at least justify it." He glances over at me. "You can say you're ridding the world of a bad person and that you'll never do it again. And you can mean that. You're doing a good thing, Quinn." Liam promises.

I glance out the window. "I'm burning down a house." I mutter. "It doesn't really feel like a good thing."

"Whether or not something is good isn't about the action itself." Liam says simply. "It's about the net outcome. You are solving a problem that karma didn't fix on its own. And I think that's rather beautiful." He smiles. "Besides, I'm not going to let you chicken out." He lifts his shirt and I see the gun sitting between his abs. "This needs to happen before Josh hurts someone else."

"Thanks for the pep talk, I guess." I furrow my brows as he pulls the van to a stop.

He nods. "Any time." Liam grabs the gun out of his waist band and I back up a little until he hands it to me. "In case things go south."

I raise a brow at him. "Who said I know how to shoot a gun?"

"You have a license and you frequent a gun range in the city often enough that I would sure fucking hope you know how to shoot." Liam smirks at me. "I don't work with anyone without doing my research on them."

"Creepy." I mutter.

"Watch it." He growls. "I have another."

I take the gun from him and tuck it into the back of my black leggings. "Won't the neighbors hear the gunshot?" I ask him.

"Yes, they will." He slides his seat back and starts typing at a speed well beyond the normal range. "Which is why it's only for emergencies. He should be out of it. I broke in and drugged every liquor bottle he has and he's been drinking consistently enough that might kill him on its own."

"You shouldn't have any problems knocking him out but if you do, I want you to have a way to save yourself." Liam says. "Coms are back on and cameras are disabled." He nods at the door. "Time to go, Quinn."

I take a deep breath and exit the van. The chill of the wind and the cold rattles through my bones in my black long sleeve shirt. I feel like a fucking burglar with my hair up in a bun, wearing all black, and stalking through the night air and I guess I kind of am.

I run through the neighborhood as fast as I can carrying this heavy ass backpack until I approach the house. "Which door is un-locked?" I ask softly through the coms.

"The front has an electronic code that I can give you, go in that way, just keep your head down." Liam responds quickly.

I make my way through the tall snow in their backyard trying to be as quiet as fucking possible. The boots are generic and will be thrown out by the morning so I was told not to worry too much about my foot prints. They are also a size larger than my feet which is making it a lot fucking harder to walk.

The house is silent on the inside and I have no way of knowing where in the house Josh is but I'm just hoping he's already knocked out from the booze. The gun sits heavy in the back of my pants as I get to the front door.

"Seven, three, nine, five." Liam says before I even ask him for the door code.

I punch in the numbers quickly and the door creaks open on loud hinges. I cringe a little at the sound. I take a couple steps inside and close the door behind me. Maybe a second passes before I feel a hard body tackle me to the ground.

I hit the tile hard, my head slamming into it and making me immediately disoriented. I let out a shriek and the questions start flooding the earpiece.

"What's happening?" Liam says clipped.

"Are you okay?" Riley's concerned voice asks.

"Quinn?" Beck's voice is a plea for me to answer.

The body on top of me flips me over and I stare up into Josh's wide deranged eyes. "Are you the one who fucking tried to drug me?" He growls, his fist coming down across my face and I let out another scream.

"I'm on my way." Beck says through the earpiece.

"Beck." Liam growls a warning. "I'm closer, I've got it covered." His voice is breathless like he's running. "Go back inside the bar with Riley."

"Liam, he's already half way down the street." Riley says. "I can't catch up with him, I'm not fast enough, what do you want me to do?"

Liam sighs. "This is what I get for helping amateurs. Gabriel is going to be so fucking pissed at me when we get back home. Let him come. If he wants to get himself arrested, fine. But Riley, stay in the bar. I don't want you anywhere near this."

Riley saying, "Yes, Sir." Comes out far too quickly, but I'm only half paying attention to their conversation because Josh has me pinned down underneath him.

"What the fuck are you doing here?" He growls.

I stay silent letting the next punch land and just trying to keep myself together. My ears are ringing softly and the headache that started when I fell is getting worse with each punch.

"*WHAT ARE YOU DOING HERE?*" He yells again.

I hear the rattling of the door handle behind me and so does Josh. He climbs off of me and turns his attention to the intrusion.

Liam comes through the door and Josh's eyes go wide as Liam towers towards him. "Get away from her and pick on someone your own size."

I scramble backwards further into the hall-way.

"Quinn, get to work." Liam orders. "I'll take care of this."

I nod and start fumbling through my back-pack but my eyes can't see straight. I can't make heads or tails of anything I'm looking at and I feel faint. I grip the sides of my head trying to put myself back together.

Glancing over I see Liam punch Josh square in the nose with an expertise that I almost envy. Josh takes a swing back and Liam ducks underneath it.

"Who the fuck are you?" Josh huffs.

Liam doesn't answer, instead he just takes another swing at Josh's head. "Quinn, the syringe." He orders as his gloved fist connects again with Josh's face.

I fumble through the bag looking for it and it takes a second but eventually I find it in the fucking bottom. I don't really know what's happening with the fight but the next time I look over, Liam has Josh in a fucking choke hold and Josh is flailing against him.

Quickly I rush over to him but I stumble and fall to the ground.

Liam sighs. "Just stay back, I've got this." He holds Josh tighter and the flailing starts to slow and slow and eventually Josh's body goes fairly limp. Liam waits another thirty seconds after that before dropping Josh to the floor.

He takes the syringe out of my hand and stabs Josh in the arm with it before squeezing down the plunger. Liam didn't tell me what was in the syringe, just that it would kill him and be untraceable. I didn't really want to ask any more questions after that.

Liam tosses the syringe into the bag before kneeling down next to me. "Look up." He says and I do. "With your eyes, Quinn, not your head. Follow my finger." He moves it back and forth, and I do my best to follow it with my eyes but my head hurts when I do. "Beckett, are you still there?"

"Yes. Is Quinn okay?" He asks over the coms and his voice feels so fucking loud.

"She has a concussion." Liam answers.

Beck growls through the comms. "I'm going to kill him."

"Already taken care of." Liam smirks.

"No." Beck comes through the door then. "I'm going to fucking kill him." He storms into the kitchen and Liam follows running after him.

"Beckett, don't do anything stupid!" Liam whisper-yells, "What happened to leaving no trace? What happened to this looking like an accident?"

He comes back down the hallway holding a knife and stands menacingly over Josh's body.

"Liam, I appreciate your help up until this point and I very well might go to jail for this, but I no longer fucking care." Beck takes a deep breath. "This mother fucker killed my sister and gave my girlfriend a concussion. I'm going to kill him."

"I can respect a crime of passion." Liam shrugs. "But I don't want any part of it." He heads to the door and turns back to Beck and me with a smile, "Good luck."

"Wait, take Quinn with you." Beck says.

"No." I argue. "I want to stay with you." I tell him.

Beck shakes his head. "You have a concussion, you need to go, firebug." He nods at the door. "Please, Quinn, go with Liam."

I look between the two of them and apparently I'm being too slow because Liam comes up to me with a sigh. He grabs my hand. "Let's go, Quinn." And then I'm being pulled out the door and away from whatever horrors unfold in that house.

Chapter Twenty Four

Beckett

I punch Josh in the face a handful of times with a growl. "You killed my fucking sister!" I scream at his passed out form.

Josh takes a gasping breath at the second punch seeming to come back from whatever had knocked him out the first time, the drugs not seeming to have taken him yet. "You're a fucking psycho." Josh spits.

"I'm the fucking psycho?" I hiss, another punch lands with my hand not holding the knife. "Fuck it, I'm not arguing with you." I take a deep shaking breath and raise the knife high above my head with both hands.

"Wait!" Josh screams.

I don't.

I bring the knife down on Josh's neck and blood squirts out onto the ground. Josh's body flops for a second before going still underneath me and I sigh in relief. "That was for Lila." I mutter, climbing off of him.

I head over to the backpack and start digging through it for the fire starters. I don't want to be here any longer than I have to be so I take the bag and start placing them around the first floor but I don't bother to go upstairs. As long as I'm able to derail my team long enough, the whole place should go up anyways.

"How's it going, Beck?" Riley asks through the coms.

"I have most of the fire starters out." I report back.

"Riley, get off this line and answer your damned phone." Liam growls. "I know you're not at the bar. Where the hell are you?"

Riley and I were never at the bar, in full honesty. She knew I wouldn't actually be able to stay away with Quinn in danger so she's sitting in my truck a few streets over in the opposite direction of where Liam parked, keeping an eye on things from over there.

Honestly, I think she worries about Liam too. She had said something about how whenever he has to go out on excursions it's rare that she's not lurking somewhere nearby just in case he needs her.

"I'm... out for a drive." She chuckles.

Liam groans exasperatedly. "I don't like how much Gianna is rubbing off on you. You need new friends."

Riley sighs. "Liam."

"Answer. Your. Phone." He says again.

I pull out the ear piece no longer wanting to be distracted by their argument. There is a pack of cigarettes in the bottom of the back-pack and I light one, blowing the smoke into the detector in the hallway just for the hell of it.

The chirping starts going off and I just laugh at it thinking how useless those damn things are if no one actually responds to them.

I walk around the house, lighting the fire starters one at a time with the lighter while I puff at my cigarette. The house slowly starts to go up in flames and I start pouring lighter fluid over everything. It reminds me of light-ing my parents house on fire, of lighting the bookstore. Bathing this town in flames and washing away its sins.

Once the fire is going strong around me I pop the ear piece in.

"Beckett!" Liam shouts. "Where the fuck are you? Dumbass taking the coms out."

"I'm here." I grumble to him as I finish the rest of my cigarette and toss it onto the carpet.

"You need to hurry up and get out of there before the place is lit up enough that neighbors see it." Liam huffs. "Leave out the back door and meet us at the van. I'm sure you know where it is."

He's right, I do know where it is. I did a lap around the block to check where they were set up before parking my truck. "What happened to not wanting any part of this?" I counter with a chuckle.

Liam sighs. "Just. Get. Out."

I spray Josh's body down in the last of the lighter fluid before listening to Liam. I head towards the back door and keep my head down as I sneak out. I run through the yards, trying to follow the tracks that Quinn left behind her as to not create a second set of foot prints.

It takes me a few minutes but eventually I reach the van and climb into the back seat. Liam glances back at me and starts to pull the van away. "You're such a dumbass." He mutters.

"Don't act like you won't do the same for me." Riley huffs through the ear piece and I can hear her driving away in the truck too.

"Whatever." Liam huffs. "Let's just get him back home so when they call him in fifteen minutes or so to come put out the fire he won't *coincidentally* be at the scene of the crime again."

The van speeds through the streets back towards my place. Quinn lays her head down on me in the backseat and it's only then that I notice her nose is bleeding. "Quinn." I whisper softly, rubbing her head. "Are you okay?" I ask her.

She tries to nod but when she does she hisses. "Everything is blurry." She mutters.

"Is she laying down?" Liam asks, glancing in the back mirror. "Don't let her pass out." He orders. "She has a concussion, you want to keep her awake. If she passes out we'll have to take her to a hospital and a hospital will have questions."

I help her get seated upright. "Quinn." I tap her face softly and her eyes open back up. I sigh in relief. "What's my name?"

"Beck." She answers.

"What's his name?" I point at Liam.

She pauses and blinks at me a little bit, her eyes seeming like they are rolling around in her head. "I don't... I don't know."

I look to Liam with some concern.

"She doesn't know me well." He assures me. "It's not abnormal for her short term memory to be affected after a concussion. Her not remembering me makes sense. She's met me a handful of times at best."

I nod but keep looking in her eyes like I will somehow see something that will make everything better or maybe worse. I honestly don't know what I'm expecting. "Quinn, do you know what month it is?"

She chews on her lip and lets out a groan.

"Stop asking her questions." Liam barks from the front seat. "Her short term memory is impaired, we already know that. Now you're just making her head hurt."

I glare at him, "I'm trying to keep her awake."

Liam's mouth clicks shut. "Continue." He mutters.

"Quinn, what month is it?" I ask her again. Her eyes flutter around in her head. "Take a few deep breaths." I order her. "In." I coach. "And out. In. And out." She does as instructed and I'm grateful that she's at least able to focus enough to do that.

After a few more minutes Liam pulls the rented van into the driveway. "Where the fuck is–" He cuts off his sentence as he sees Riley pull into the driveway in my truck. He climbs out of the van. "Where the hell were you!?" He screams.

Quinn's hands go to her head covering her ears as she hisses. "Loud." She whimpers out. "Everything is loud."

I unbuckle and help her out of the truck. "Let's go inside." But it is of course at that moment that my phone starts ringing. I check the caller ID and see it's Albert. I answer on the second ring. "Yeah?"

"There's a fire at Josh Ericson's house." Albert says. "You wouldn't happen to know anything about that would you?" He asks, with a chuckle.

"I know that karma is a bitch." I shrug into the phone. "But other than that, nothing."

Albert laughs. "I'm sure that's true, chief. Either way, we'll need you out here pronto to help put it out."

I nod. "I'm on my way." I tell him before hanging up the phone. I start to help Quinn out of the car but Liam stops me.

"Riley and I got her." He promises.

"Thank you.," I tell him, "For everything."

"Yeah whatever." He shrugs. "You better go."

I fly out of the van and Riley passes me my keys as I hop into the cab of my truck. I take off back the exact way we just came feeling like I'm doing loops for no damned reason other than to confuse people. This is some bullshit.

It takes me a solid ten minutes to get back to Josh's house and when I get there the place is more of an inferno than I left it.

Fire flies out of the windows on the second floor as members of my team start pulling up to the scene and putting on their turnout gear. Albert approaches me first as I park blocking off the road for anyone else who might try and come down the street.

"I was just about to send someone in there and check for survivors, but I did a tempera-ture reading and it's too hot for that." Albert smiles. "Wouldn't be safe to risk someone for what's likely an empty house, don't you think, chief?"

I nod. "Agreed." I tell him, pulling my turnout gear from the back of the truck. "Focus on making sure the fire doesn't spread to the surrounding buildings before actually putting the fire out. I can already see it travelling in the yard even with the snow."

Albert salutes. "We're on it."

Bridget and Detective Clark have been poking around my scene for almost the entire time it's been up in flames. It's been over an hour at this point and while we *almost* have the fire put out there are still flames licking up in random places. We've more than deemed it unsafe to go inside despite Clark's multiple attempts.

I understand to an extent. Josh and Clark were partners so the thought that his partner might be dead in a house fire is understandably upsetting. But his partner is also a massive fucking douche who deserved to get stabbed in the fucking neck and Clark is trampling all over my scene so my sympathy is starting to run thin.

"Clark!" I bark at him as he approaches the house. "If I see you get within one hundred feet of the fire one more time I'm calling your police chief and getting you removed from the scene."

My phone starts ringing in the pants of my turnout gear. I make sure that Clark starts to back away first, which he does, before I answer it. The number comes across the screen as unknown and my stomach drops. "Hello?"

Riley smiles softly through the phone. "Don't panic."

"I don't like this already." I mutter.

"Liam and our pilot are flying Quinn to a hospital out of state. He couldn't take her to a local hospital for the obvious reasons." Riley says. "Quinn passed out shortly after you left and Liam decided with how much she was bleeding from her nose and the gash on her cheek that she probably needed stitches any-ways."

I nod numbly. "Thank you for letting me know."

"I'm waiting for you at your house so we can have another bonfire. We need to burn your clothes and her clothes and anything from the scene. Try and get here soon. None of us really considered you're still wearing the same thing. Wear your turnout gear back if you can drive in it."

"I need to be with Quinn." I tell her.

"She's safe." Riley promises. "I know Liam is kind of terrifying at best and at worst..." She trails off. "My point is, Quinn is more than safe with him. He protects his own. He will make sure nothing happens to her, I promise. If for no other reason than I refuse to find a new editor. She has to be okay." Her tone is soft and hopeful.

"Okay." I tell her watching my team work to put out the fire. "I need to let you go, we are almost done here."

"I'll see you in a little bit."

"Taking a phone call in the middle of a fire?" Clark sneers at me as he and Bridget approach from one of the nearby police cruisers.

I glare at him and sigh. "Can I help you with something, officer?"

"Detective." He corrects. "And I want to be able to go inside the home to investigate the fire. It's almost out, we want to check for bodies."

"I haven't been able to do a check on the structure yet to ensure that it's stable." I tell him. "If I let you walk in there and the ceiling caves in on you, I lose my fucking job and you lose a lot more. So you'll excuse me if I want to do my due diligence before I let you investigate, *detective*."

Clark looks like he's about to go off but Bridget steps in. "Let me talk to him." She tells Clark. "We are old friends." He bristles but takes a step back. Apparently that wasn't good enough for Bridget. "Go wait in the car, you're too close to this anyways."

He bristles but he seems to respect her so he listens and goes back towards the car.

Bridget shifts on her feet and glances back at the house. "Did you do this?" She asks outright.

I shake my head. "How could I have? I got here after the house was already on fire. I was at home with Quinn."

She straightens a little at the mention of her sister. "Don't drag Quinn into your bullshit, Beckett." She growls at me. "I know you did this. And–"

I cut her off. "Do you have any proof of that, Detective O'Brady?"

"No." She whispers.

"Are you making an official accusation?"

She stares me down for a second, seeming to try and size me up. "How involved was my little sister in your evening plans?"

"Heavily." I grit out.

Bridget sighs. "Quinn." She kicks her head back. "No, I'm not making an official accusation." She surrenders and I breathe out a sigh of relief. "But I will be keeping an eye on you.

I shrug as I start to walk away, going back to check on Albert and the crew. "That will be hard to do when I'm in New York."

Quinn

I know I went to the hospital because Liam and Riley told me I did, but I don't remember a second of it. The next thing I do remember is laying on Beck's couch watching him pack his stuff into boxes. Everything in here kind of smells like smoke and I can't tell if that's from cigarettes or something else.

My eyes trace nothing on the ceiling, and I could have sworn I was feeling better today, but I'm also sporting a raging headache that is making me think that might not be true. The concussion was fairly minor according to the doctors and there was no internal bleeding or anything major to worry about. They just prescribed bed rest and not to do anything too mentally strenuous which means no editing for me for at least a week or two.

Riley and Liam went back to New York this morning. They had plans already for the New Year, they are going to some bar or club with Madison and a few other author friends of Riley's.

I go to push up off the couch to help Beck pack but he waves me off. "You should be laying down." Beck purrs, wrapping an arm around my waist and guiding me back towards the couch.

"I'm fine." I argue back, pulling away from him. "Let me help you pack."

"Bug, you are definitely not fine." Beck argues. "I can pack on my own, I promise. Please just go lay back down."

I don't, instead moving over to where the boxes are sitting in the corner and starting to put one together. "My head hurts, not my body." I tell him, taping the box together. "And this is a big thing you're doing for me, I want to help."

Beck takes the tape from me and tapes the bottom of the box that I put together for him before taking it out of my hands. "If you really want to do something for me you would go lay down."

"I've been laying down all morning." I argue.

Beck sets the box down and brushes some of the hair away from my face. He leans into me. "Quinn, I need you to feel better for New Years because I have some plans for you."

I tilt my head at him. "What kind of plans?"

"The kind that involves no clothing and something I didn't pack away into one of these boxes yet." He purrs. "Now go lay down."

I groan. "Fine." I mutter as I turn to head towards the couch the doorbell rings. A look passes between the two of us. "Are you expecting someone?"

Beck shakes his head. "No." I move to get the door but he waves me off. "Go lay down Quinn, I've got it." He peaks through the pinhole and quickly backs away from the door. He grabs me by the hand and starts dragging me back towards his bedroom.

"What the fuck is happening?" I ask him as he rifles through one of the boxes.

"I'm looking for my gun." Beck answers as if that's enough information?

"Why?" I question, grabbing my purse off the bed and pulling my small beretta out of it. "Who the hell was out there?" I jump a little when the doorbell rings again but this time it's followed up by a very loud and aggressive knocking.

"I don't fucking know, but they are wearing a mask and holding a gun." He glances back over at me. "Where the hell did you get that?"

I hold up my purse. "I live in New York. Do you have any idea how much crime there is in that city? The statistics are scary at best."

Beck turns his attention back to the box and pulls out his own gun which is quite a bit bigger than mine, not that size really matters. "Stay here. I don't want you getting hurt."

I scoff. "Beck, I can more than handle my-self." I promise. "And it's a lot easier to be two people against a lone gunman than one on one."

He thinks about it for a second, his brows furrowing like he's not happy with my logic even if he understands it. "I-" Whatever he was going to say is cut off by a loud banging coming from the door.

Both of us rush from the room, knowing better than to be caught cornered. Beck makes some motions indicating for me to stay hidden at the hallway's turn point so no one will see me from the door.

I stay where I'm told as he makes his way over to the front door and unlocks it. He stands behind the door and has his gun pointed down. I keep an eye over my shoulder as the door swings open. Beck points his gun at the man's head. "Freeze" He growls.

The man's about to make a move, about to try something but I move out from the corner. "He said freeze." I hiss and the gunman goes still.

His frame is on the taller side but not taller than Beck. He's wearing a balaclava and while I have no idea who exactly he is off hand it's clear he's a man.

"Drop the gun." Beck orders.

The man slowly lowers to the ground and sets the gun down, Beck follows him with his pistol staying locked on the man's head. Once the gun is down Beck kicks it away from the man. "Quinn." Beck says, nodding to the gun.

I approach slowly, before squatting down to pick it up. I keep my eyes trained on the man the whole time as he watches me back through the mask.

Everything happens so quickly I almost don't have enough time to react. The man turns on Beck. He pushes the gun upwards in Beck's hand and Beck fires but just a little too late as the man ducks down and out of the shot. The shot embeds in the wall and the man grabs the gun off Beck, flipping it around on him. He's about to shoot when Beck jumps back and my instincts kick in.

I aim my gun at the man's chest, knowing that's the easiest target, even with him turned to the side, and fire. The bullet feels like it flies through the air in slow motion as I watch Beck move out of the gunman's shot.

The man goes down, his hands dropping the gun as he keels over, grasping his side. Beck kicks the gun away from the man and bends down to grab the mask off of him. I approach slowly, not recognizing the man and trying to ascertain why the hell he came and attacked us.

"Clark." Beck mutters, his tone solemn. "Why?"

"You killed my partner." He grits out, writhing on the ground. "I know you killed Josh and I don't want this life without him. I was never planning to come back from this..." He groans.

I shake my head. "Why do you care so much?" I question, chewing on my lip. I tuck my gun into the back of my pants.

"He was my *partner*." Clark emphasizes. "We've been together since the police academy. And I have no desire to go on without him. He never loved Alexa." The man chokes out.

"It wasn't a mistress." I mutter.

Clark shakes his head. "There were never any mistresses. Just me." He takes a shuddering breath before his chest goes still.

"Beck what the hell do we do now?"

He stares down at Clark. "He broke in." Beck shrugs. "Whatever his reason, he broke in, we had every right to do what we did."

I shake my head again. "You know no one is going to see it that way."

Beck nods. "Yeah, I know."

"Do we call Liam?" I ask.

Beck's eyes haven't left Clark this whole time. He takes a deep breath and finally pulls his gaze. "No, Liam had to have known about this and didn't warn us. I don't want to go any further down that rabbit hole. We need to-"

His phone starts to ring in his pocket, not Beck's phone... Clark's phone.

Beck crouches down and flips the phone to show me the *Unknown* number scrawled across it. Beck answers the call and puts it on speaker, the voice is immediately recognizable after yesterday.

"His location history is deleted so no one will find out he was there. We can call this another favor," Liam purrs. "And yes, I knew about him, but no, I didn't think he would do this. Burn the remains and let's put this whole thing to bed." And then the call ends without another word.

Beck tosses the phone on the ground and smashes it with his heel. "Prick."

My phone goes off.

Unknown: I heard that.

I turn the phone around so Beck can see it.

He groans. "This is what I get for making deals with the devil." He mutters.

My phone dings again, this time with just a smirking emoji. I go to show Beck again but he waves me off.

"Leave him go, we have shit to do." Beck says, starting to pull Clark out the door. I stare after him, my mind trying to catch up with what the fuck just happened. If someone had told me before I left for Vermont that I would spend part of my holidays watching my boyfriend drag away the dead body of the man I killed I wouldn't have believed them.

"Quinn." Beck barks. "A little help here?"

I shake my head. "Right."

I watch the bonfire smoke filling the night air long after Clark is gone. Beck just kept it burning and burning and burning and burning. I sit on a log a few feet away just staring into the mess of red and orange and yellow flames.

Beck insisted that we burn our clothes which I was more than a little against because I really fucking loved this sweater but he stripped it off of me and burned it anyways. I'm still pissed about that.

Jackass owes me a new sweater.

My eyes stare into the abyss, hazing over and I can't tell if that is because of the concussion or if I'm dissociating. The chill of the wind is rattling through my bones even in my coat, but I don't want to go back inside. I don't want to go look at the blood we still need to bleach away.

Beck tosses another log onto the fire apparently intent on continuing the burn in spite of it being far from necessary now. I want to go to bed, but I won't go without him.

He walks over to me and takes a seat on the log beside me. He pulls me into his arms and it almost helps with how cold I am, but not really. "Quinn, you should go lay down."

I shake my head. "I'm fine here." I tell him, but I don't look away from the fire.

Beck takes my chin in his hand and turns my face to look at him. He grabs my hands and rubs up and down my fingers. "You're freezing." He whispers, pushing to his feet to stand up. He sweeps me up into his arms without another word. "You need to get inside."

I want to protest, I want to argue, but everything is cold and I'm beyond exhausted. So instead I let Beck carry me back towards the blood stained house and over the only remains of the man I killed.

I'm not sure I'm ever going to understand how people cope with something like this.

Liam has said I was doing the right thing by killing Josh because he was a bad person... Clark wasn't a bad person.

He did a bad thing, but he wasn't a bad person.

What I did was wrong. And I can't fix it.

I start sobbing softly into Beck's shoulder as he carries me into the bedroom. He lays me down on the bed and crouches down next to me to pull me into his arms. Beck shushes me softly, but it doesn't help.

"I'm a bad person." I mutter into his chest. "I did a bad thing. I'm a bad person."

"Quinn, I don't think it's ever that simple." Beck whispers against my forehead. I want to follow his logic, but I just keep crying. He tilts my head up and kisses me softly. "You need to get some sleep and you'll feel better in the morning." Beck promises softly.

I shake my head. "I don't..."

Beck just shushes me, climbing into bed beside me to hold me. "Go to sleep, firebug." He purrs and in the comfort of his arms, I do.

Chapter Twenty Six

Quinn

"Quinn, I'm telling you he's dangerous." Bridget pleads through the phone. "Please, everything that happened with Josh and now Clark is gone right behind him. It's–"

"Something you'd been told by your police chief not to worry about?" I question and there is a silence on the line. "Bridge, I appreciate you looking out for me, but I know who Beck is."

Bridget sighs. "That's part of what I'm worried about. I don't like that he got you involved in whatever the hell all of this was." Bridget's tone is soft and full of concern, but honestly I'm just annoyed that she doesn't think I can make my own decisions. "Whatever downward spiral Beckett is on... I don't want him dragging you down with him."

"It's fine, Bridget." I huff. "And the less you and everyone else asks questions the finer it will be. I can handle myself. I promise. So don't worry about me." I try to soften my voice to make it sound reassuring instead of frustrated, but I don't know how much it works.

I lean back on the couch, staring at my laptop. Even before Bridget called, editing wasn't going all that well. I'm probably going to have to go over this again in a week or so with fresh eyes.

"What about dad?" Bridget asks. "You've been over at Beckett's for days. Dad wants to see you while you're here, Quinn."

I run a hand through my hair. "I will be over tomorrow for New Years Day and we will stop by before we leave for New York."

"With Beckett, I'm sure." Bridget mutters.

"He's my boyfriend." I state plainly. "If you want me there, he'll come with." Beck comes down the hallway, leaning against the wall he smiles at me. "We're kind of a package deal now." I chuckle, smiling back at him.

"Fine." Bridget says in a way that makes it very clear it's not actually fine, but I don't think

I really care. "I've got to get back to Adriane. I'll see you tomorrow. Love you." She bites out the words but I know she means them anyways.

"Love you too." I tell her, hanging up the phone and setting it down on the couch as Beck starts to prowl towards me. I move my laptop and go to stand.

"It's almost midnight." Beck purrs, wrapping a hand around my middle and pulling me in towards him. "I have some ideas on how we should ring in the New Year."

I nod, already liking where this is going. "What kind of ideas?"

He pushes me up against the wall beside the couch and raises my hands above my head. "Keep them still, and I will give you a reward. Let them down and you'll be punished." He says, clearly laying out my new set of rules. "Understand, firebug?"

I nod. "Yes." I respond breathlessly.

He taps the side of my cheek. "Good." His lips go to mine in an instant, licking and sucking at my bottom lip before pressing a kiss to me. His mouth works against mine in a way that feels harmonious and I kiss him back feverishly.

"Beck." I moan into our kiss. My hands want to go to his shoulders, to his chest, to his cock, but I keep them up as I was told.

His hands on the other hand start roving my body. He finds the bottom of my sweater and slips his fingers underneath of it. He palms my breast softly before rolling his thumb over my nipple.

I take a shuddering breath and my head tilts back as I push myself close to him. I want more. I need more. I need him.

He keeps kissing me through his motions as he slowly moves his hand over to my other breast and repeats the roll with his thumb. "I think you need this sweater off, Quinn." He purrs.

"Yes." I breathe out.

His hands go to the bottom and he starts to pull it over my head but he takes his time drawing out the motion intentionally in a way that's making me squirm. I want his hands back on my body and off this fucking sweater, but the sweaters getting to have all the fun right now.

After what feels like a short eternity he gets it up over my head and then quickly throws it on the ground. His hands immediately go back to my body, this time running softly over my sides.

My hands flinch wanting to touch him back, but I think better of it. I don't know what a punishment from Beck would look like, but I'm not sure I want to know. I'd rather get the reward.

"Having trouble there?" He purrs into my ear.

"A little." I answer honestly.

Beck runs a thumb over my jaw. "If it becomes too much, and you need an out, tap the wall three times and you can let your hands down, no punishment, no reward. We can just stop." He promises.

"So a safe gesture?"

He nods. "I tend to like them better than safe words." He starts kissing softly at my neck and I let out a breathless giggle. "Besides, sometimes it can be hard to talk when you're in sub space." He grabs my chin and nods my head for me. "Isn't that right, firebug?"

I chew on my lip as I watch him with wide eyes.

"Do you want more or do you need to stop, Quinn?" Beck asks, his fingers playing softly on my jaw.

"More." I respond without an ounce of hesitation.

Beck smiles. "That's my girl." His finger skirt up my arms, almost like he's tickling them and they twitch at the sensation. He's smirking wildly as I shift back and forth on my feet. He goes up and down my arms a few times before starting to move his fingers lower, across my chest, then my stomach, then between my legs.

He leans into me and starts kissing me again while his hand goes under my leggings. He runs his fingers over my slit and hums, "You're wet." Beck pushes his fingers inside of me.

"Yes." I nod.

"Good." He uses the other hand to roughly yank my leggings down my body. I stumble a little before righting myself. He gets the leggings all the way off and spreads my legs.

Beck's fingers plunge in and out of my pussy in long strokes. I roll my hips towards him but he uses his opposite hand to pin my pelvis to the wall. My hands fall back, resting against the wall, my arms are starting to get tired and are a little tingly from being up so long. I flex my fingers trying to fight through the muscle exhaustion.

He keeps fingering me, but eventually my arms start to droop. "Keep them up, Quinn." He purrs, taking the hand that was holding my pelvis and using it to grab my wrist. Beck pushes them up and holds them for a second which does provide some relief, but I'm still starting to wear thin.

"I'm trying." I whimper.

He nods, kissing my cheek. "I know, bug, and you're doing so well." He praises. "Just a little bit longer and I'll let you bring them down." His thumb rolls over my clit and I find myself moaning into his shoulder.

Beck keeps massaging my clit and working his fingers in and out of me. His tongue swirls around mine and he leans back in to kiss me again and I feel beyond overwhelmed.

My mind briefly considers tapping out, knowing I have the option is a comfort, but not one I need right now. I want more even if I'm struggling. I want to give him what he wants, but it's good to know I have an out.

Beck brings my body quickly to the edge with his fingers, working me masterfully like an expert harpist plucking at every correct string to make the perfect melody. I'm more than grateful to have a partner who knows what they are doing.

"I want you to finish on my fingers." Beck orders. "And once you do, you can let your arms rest on my shoulders. Don't drop them all the way."

I nod.

"Good girl." He keeps going, his fingers bringing me to crescendo. "You're doing so good." He praises. "I want to feel you squeeze my fingers when you cum. Be a good girl and do that for me, Quinn."

I take a few deep breaths and I feel the orgasm start to wash over me in warm waves. I cry out before biting down on my lip trying to stabilize myself. My whole body quakes against the wall, every inch of my mind completely mush as I lower my arms onto Beck's shoulders.

"Wrap your legs around me." He orders, lifting me up between him and the wall. I do and he pulls me into his arms and starts carrying me towards the bedroom.

Beck tosses me down on the bed and grabs something off the dresser that I didn't see what it was. He bends me over, face down ass up and I hear him unzip his pants.

A few seconds pass before I start hearing a buzzing coming from behind me. I glance back and see a vibrating cock ring wrapped around Beck's dick. He pushes his cock between my legs and I feel fucking electric. Every nerve ending is on fire in the best possible way.

My eyes roll into the back of my head as I push myself further onto Beck's dick, needing more. I was already sensitive from my orgasm, having his cock shaking inside of me is a whole new level of overwhelmed but I want it, I want more.

Beck smacks my ass hard and I scream into the mattress. He grabs my hips and starts to roll them on his cock as he pushes in and out of me in one fluid motion.

"More." I beg. "More, more, More."

He obliges and continues to fuck me into the mattress. His hands grip deeply into my sides and for a second I focus on that sensation to try and ground myself from the vibrations between my legs.

I know I'm going to be sore tomorrow but I don't fucking care, it's worth it. He's worth everything. I... I think... I think I love him...

It might be way too soon. It might be a cliche to tell him that I love him while he's balls fucking deep inside of me, but I do. I love him and I want him to fucking know...

"Beck?" I moan, glancing over my shoulder.

He slows down. "Yes, Quinn?" He pulls out and flips me over onto my back. His eyes find mine and something in them must see how I feel. "Is there something you need to say, firebug?"

I nod.

He pushes back inside of me, this time with me laying on my back. Beck grabs my shoulder and pulls down so he's fucking me deeper than I really even thought possible. "What is it?"

"I..." I mutter. "I lo..." I shake my head trying to figure out how the fuck to say this.

"Do you want me to go first, Quinn?"

I nod again, this time more desperate.

He leans down to whisper in my ear, "I love you, Quinn."

"I love you too, Beck." I moan out.

Beck presses his lips to mine as he continues to fuck me. His cock shakes between my legs and I hear him groan. "Fuck." He grunts and he pushes fully inside of me.

My eyes go a little wide as Beck pulls out breathlessly. He rolls the cock ring off his dick before turning it off. "Did you finish already?" I ask a little surprised.

He nods. "Quinn, I've been waiting to hear you say those words since I was in high school." He chuckles. "You'll have to excuse the quick draw."

I push upright and chuckle back. "I guess that's fair enough." I run a hand through my hair and he pulls me into his arms.

His hand grabs my chin again and tilts my face up towards his. "I love you, Quinn." He whispers.

I nod back. "I love you too." I chew on my lip.

"What is it?" Beck asks.

"I don't want you to find your own place when we get to Manhattan." I tell him. "I... I want us to find a place together."

Beck tilts his head to the side. "Are you sure?"

"Yeah." I lean in to kiss him. "Yeah, I'm sure."

He smiles. "I'd like that." Beck pulls his phone out of his pocket. "It's ten after midnight." He tells me, flipping the phone screen around. "Happy New Year, firebug."

"Best New Years I've ever had." I smile at him. "Happy New Year, Beck."

Chapter Twenty Seven

Quinn

I canceled my flight back but Beck rented a U-Haul that we will have through the end of the week. I have a storage unit in my apartment building that Madison and I don't really use so we should have plenty of room to put all of his random crap while we are looking for a place.

Bridget offered to help move, surprisingly, but I have a feeling it was just an excuse to get to see Beck's place and check for evidence so we declined. I don't really want her snooping around anymore than I'm sure she already will when we are gone.

We got the U-Haul loaded up last night and I promised my family that I would drop by and see them this morning before we left. Honestly, I've been dreading it more than I wish I was.

I sigh, as Beck pulls the truck into the driveway of my parents' house. It still hasn't been shoveled but enough tracks have run over it that it's easier to pull in and out of now.

He puts the truck into park and goes to get out but stops when he sees that I don't move. "Quinn?" He asks, shaking my shoulder lightly.

I stare straight ahead at my dad's old truck, covered in more snow, no one having used it since I went to the bookshop almost two weeks ago now. "I don't know if I can do this."

"We don't have to stay long." Beck promises. "We can just drop in, say bye, and then get on the road with the U-Haul."

I nod, but I know that's probably not true. "I just... I wish my relationship with them wasn't like this. I wish that we were close and that I didn't..." I stop, shaking my head. "Never mind, let's just go inside." I go to open the door but Beck grabs my arm.

"Wish you didn't, what, Quinn?" He asks.

I huff a humorless laugh. "Nothing. Just, we should go inside." I try to get out of the truck again but Beck doesn't let me.

"No, tell me." He tilts my chin to look at him. "You can tell me anything, Quinn." He moves in to kiss me. "I love you, and nothing is ever going to change that. So tell me."

I sigh, chewing on my lip and put to words what I've spent years trying to pretend I didn't feel. "I wish I didn't resent them for staying here." I whisper like it's my best kept secret... it was. "I wish I could make peace with that they decided they didn't want more from life than what this town has to offer, but I can't."

"Why not?"

"Because it makes me feel like something is wrong with me!" I shriek, before taking a deep breath and trying to settle myself. "What... what's wrong with me that I couldn't just be happy where I was? Why did I have to go find something else? Why couldn't I have just been like Bridget and stayed here?"

He takes my chin in his hand. "Quinn, nothing is wrong with you." He wipes away some of my tears with his thumb. "They didn't experience the trauma that we did in this town. They've only ever had good things happen to them here. They never had something driving them to leave."

I play with my thumbs in my lap. "I just wish things were different." I lean my forehead against his. "I just wish they had come with me."

Beck nods. "But they didn't." He responds. "They keep asking you to come back to a past that only ever hurt you, but none of them are willing to move towards your present that's never been anything but welcoming."

"I just... I feel like they don't understand me."

"They don't." Beck agrees and I don't know if I was expecting that to make me feel better, but it didn't. "But I do. I understand you, Quinn. And that's why I never would have asked you to move back here for me. That's why I always was going to move with you. This place is hell for both of us."

"So then..." I glance at the door, "Does that mean we don't have to go inside?"

Beck shakes his head. "No, bug, we have to go inside." He says and I sigh. "You need to say goodbye to them."

"Or I could just run." I whisper.

"How well did running from me work the last time?" He chuckles.

I grumble a little. "Fine." I mutter, getting out of the truck. My heeled boots shuffle through the snow trying to follow the tracks already made so I don't sink in and get stuck.

When I get around to his side of the truck, Beck takes my hand and helps me over towards the front porch. We climb the steps together and I'm grateful to have him by my side this time.

I knock on the front door. I almost turn and bolt, but Beck is still holding my hand so I know that's not an option. He would grab me if I did and probably in a way that Bridget would be rather upset about if she saw it.

Bridget opens the door and smiles. "Quinn!" She blanks Beck like he's not even there as she moves in to hug me. "It's good to see you." She smiles, taking the hand that Beck just had and using it to pull me through the door.

The nerves in my stomach dance around, making nausea roll through my gut as I'm dragged inside towards the kitchen. Beck follows the two of us, closing the door behind him.

"We can't stay long," I tell her. "We have to get on the road."

Bridget frowns. "Why do you always do that?"

"Bridge." I chide.

She rolls her eyes. "Fine, whatever, stay as long as you can." As we get into the kitchen she moves to a large mixing bowl in the center of the island. "Adriane and I were about to roll out cookies." She tilts the bowl and shows the mass amounts of sugar cookie dough. "Come help."

"Actually, I need a minute with your sister." My dad says, and I just now notice he was sitting at the counter. He pushes up to his feet. "Play nice with Beckett, Bridget. We'll be back in a minute." My dad starts down the hallway and nods for me to follow.

Beck has to just about push me after him, but I start walking and head towards the living room. My dad sits down in one of the arm chairs by the fireplace and I pick the seat across from him.

The Christmas tree is still up in the living room and probably will be for a few more days until my sister and Adriane get a chance to take it down. Snow falls outside the windows and my eyes train on that not knowing what to make of my father pulling me aside alone.

He sighs, "Quinn." He starts and nerves jump through me. "I just want you to know that I'm proud of you."

I blink at him confused. "What?"

"I know what happened." He answers simply. "Probably more than you think and..." My father leans in. "Despite what your sister might say about it, that son of a bitch more than had it coming. So for whatever part you played in it. I'm proud of you."

I shake my head. "I don't know what you mean." I deny on instinct. A beat of silence passes between the two of us before I break it again, "But thanks. That actually means a lot."

My dad smiles. "And I'll learn to get used to Beckett." He shrugs. "If he makes you happy..."

"He does."

My father nods. "Then that's all that matters. That's the same thing I told your sister when she brought home Adriane." He glances towards the kitchen. "At the end of the day, who you spend your life with is your choice, not mine."

"And even though I may not like him very much now." My father continues. "I know he kept you safe in that house and that... that's what matters to me."

"Thanks dad." I smile at him.

"But seriously, couldn't you have just picked a nice girl like your sister." He chuckles.

I laugh back. "I'm straight, dad. I'm sure."

He sighs. "I'll figure out how to make peace with that. Besides, your mother, she always liked Beckett. She thought I was too hard on him when you were younger."

"Really?" I ask with wide eyes.

My father nods. "She would have approved. And I... well I probably should have trusted her judgement." He looks off into the fireplace lost in thought for a moment before coming back. "I miss your mother."

I nod. "I miss her too."

"She... she was always better at keeping the family together, and I know your sister is trying but... things just aren't the same without her around."

I reach out to hold his hand. "I know." I whisper softly.

"Do you remember, one Christmas when we were probably about in middle school, mom got us phones and didn't tell you?" I ask.

My dad nods. "At the time, I was furious. I had explicitly told her not to."

"Yeah, but do you also remember texting us both Happy New Year for the first time?" I ask.

"Yes, I remember that too." He smiles. "We had some good holidays back in the day. Your mother's chocolate chip cookie recipe is still my favorite." I chuckle and he looks at me confused. "What?"

"Can I let you in on a secret mom told me?" I whisper quietly and he nods. "She used the recipe on the back of the chocolate chip bag and just switched the teaspoon of vanilla for a tablespoon."

My father's eyes go wide. "You're kidding!" He laughs. "I've tried so many chocolate chip cookie recipes since her passing and I had never been able to figure it out."

I nod. "Yup. Family secret." I smirk. "She let me in on it when I was in high school."

"Your mother always was sneaky. But that was part of what I loved about her. She was the best at planning surprise parties and no one was ever able to predict what she would get them for birthdays." He beams. "She got together the money to open the bookshop without me even knowing. It was amazing. One day she just told me, 'Quit your job, we're following our dreams.' And that was that."

A tinge of sadness passes through the room.

"The insurance money came in." He says. "But rebuilding won't be the same without her. I... I'm actually thinking about selling the bookstore."

My eyes go wide. "To who?"

My father leans in and whispers. "Adriane. Don't tell her, it's a surprise."

I'm more than a little surprised by that and honestly not sure how I feel about it but in the end I just say, "She'll love it."

He pushes to his feet. "We better get back in the kitchen before your sister comes looking for us." I stand up too and he goes to hug me. "I love you, Quinn."

"I love you too, dad."

Chapter Twenty Eight

Quinn

Beck pulls the truck up to the curb in the loading/unloading zone outside our building. Immediately people are honking at him annoyed as they zoom around the side of the truck going way too fucking fast. It takes a solid minute for the traffic to clear up enough for him to get out and by that time Madison and... Dylan are downstairs.

His red hair is shaggy but not in an unkept way, more like it was styled that way. He smiles at me clearly already trying to get on my good side and when he does his freckles crinkle up on his pale face.

I climb out of the truck. "Fuck you." I point at Dylan before going in to hug Madison. "And I've missed you." I smiled at her before pulling back. "But seriously, why is he back in our lives?"

She waves me off and heads towards Beckett who is opening the back of the truck. "Problem for another day, Quinn. Right now just be grateful, him being here means we don't have to lift the heavy stuff."

I sigh as I look at the man who broke my best friend's heart. I want to punch him in the fucking face, but that would only hurt Madison.

"Quinn." Dylan smiles at me softly.

"Save it." I grumble, heading back towards the truck. Madison is right, Dylan is a tomorrow problem. Today I just need to focus on getting my boyfriend moved into our place.

Madison and jackass start taking some of the boxes that are labeled upstairs and head inside. I climb into the back of the truck with Beck and start to help him sort through his stuff.

Once they are out of earshot, Beck wraps an arm around my waist and pulls me into him. "Madison is smart, she'll be okay."

"Madison isn't who I'm worried about." I tell him, glancing after them. I sigh and lean in to kiss him. "But today isn't about them, it's about us."

Beck smiles and puts his hands on both sides of my face. He presses me up against the wall of the truck as he kisses me deeply. I pull back chuckling softly as he moves to pick up another one of the upstairs boxes. "Want to show me where we'll be living for the time being?"

I nod excitedly. "Yeah." I mutter, picking up another one of the boxes. I hop back out of the truck and start to head inside my building.

Beck stops on the sidewalk looking around at the city beyond. "It's... so big here." He mutters in soft awe. "I didn't expect everything to be this big."

"Never been to New York?" I ask with a chuckle as I move through the propped open door.

He follows behind me. "I've maybe been outside of our home town, five times." He chuckles softly. "So no, I've never been to New York."

"You're in for a surprise then." I press the button for the elevator. "Wait until you see the view from upstairs."

When the doors open to the elevator I see Dylan's back with Madison pressed up against the wall, his hand above her head boxing her in as she stares up into his eyes. I clear my throat and they both promptly exit, heading out towards the truck.

"Problem for another day." Beck reminds me as he walks onto the elevator. "What floor?"

I smile. "Thirty six."

His eyes go a little wide. "I don't think I've ever been that high up in a building." His hand goes to press the button, but it hovers over it for a moment in hesitation. He hits the button anyways after a second though.

"It's not as bad as you think." I promise as the elevator starts to take us upwards towards our floor. "It's mostly just a really nice view and you only occasionally feel the building sway.

He stares at me. "Please tell me that's a joke."

I swallow a little and he looks like he's about to run screaming from the building. "They are like that on purpose." I rush to tell him. "Buildings over a certain height, they make them sway in the wind so they... okay I don't know the exact reason, but I freaked out about it too when I first moved here. I promise it's normal."

Beck takes a deep breath, clearly trying to steady himself. "I'm just going to have to take your word for it." The elevator doors open and he takes a step into the hallway. "I trust you, Quinn." I follow after him. "Which one?" He nods at the three doors in the hallway.

I head towards the last one at the end of the hall. "This one." I tell him, turning the handle, knowing it was still unlocked from Madison. I push the door open and smile as I take in my home. I had missed it here. Being away for so long is miserable. Maybe next year we will only do a week for the holidays.

Beck and I walk inside and he sets the box down next to the other ones that Madison and Dylan put in the living room. He slowly walks towards the floor length windows, his eyes staring out at the city. I'm a little surprised he gets close enough to touch them, I didn't touch the windows until I had been in this building for a month.

I put my box down and come up next to him. "What do you think?" I ask softly.

He looks to me, "Beautiful." He smiles. "Just like you, Quinn."

I smile back. "I hope you'll love this city as much as I do." I whisper softly, more to myself than to him.

He takes me in his arms again, "I will." He promises. "Because you love it. And I love you, Quinn. Besides," He turns to look out the window, "This might be the most amazing view I've ever seen in my entire life."

I laugh softly and push myself into his chest. "I love you too." I whisper into his jacket.

Beck tilts my chin up to him and kisses me deeply. He swirls his tongue around mine as they dance back and forth in our mouths. His hands start roving down and under my coat.

I grab his arm and I'm about to drag him away into my bedroom when Madison clears her throat from over by the door. I glance up at her holding a box and remember that we probably shouldn't just leave the truck downstairs indefinitely unattended. We are in a mostly safe neighborhood, but still.

I pull Beck out the door like that was always my plan... it wasn't, and we head back towards the elevator. I press the button again and it ar–

rives instantly. We get inside and Beck pushes me up against the wall.

He brushes some of my red curls away from my face as he stares down at me, his other hand drifting down to my hip.

I lean past him to hit the button for the first floor. The doors close and he presses his lips to mine in the privacy. I moan into his lips and his hand finds my ass.

He cups it, pulling me close to him as the elevator carries us down back towards the main floor. Beck pulls away. "How's your head?" He asks, kissing my forehead.

"I think you'd have to answer that question." I smirk.

Beck looks a little confused then he chuckles. "I mean because of the concussion, firebug. But I do like where your mind is at." He smirks.

I laugh softly. "It's fine now. I feel a lot better. The first few days were rough, but now I just have fog occasionally."

He nods. "That's good."

The doors open behind us and he walks us back out to the truck hand in hand. We pull a few more boxes out of the back and start to head back towards the elevator.

He doesn't speak again until the doors close. "Thank you, Quinn." He smiles at me. "For being with me even after all the hell that I put you through."

I shake my head. "I... I should have been honest all those years ago. I should have just testified and you never would have had to go that far." I chew on my lip. "Lila deserved a better best friend than me."

Beck looks at me softly. "Quinn, you helped murder her killer. Lila had the best friend she ever could have asked for." The doors open again and he guides me back to the apartment.

We pass Madison and Dylan again and I very much wonder what took them so long to get back to the elevator, but I choose not to ask that question. We set the boxes down in the apartment and Beck stops again to look out at the view.

Snow starts falling down from the sky and I smile watching it start to patter against the windows. Beck stares at the snow and smiles. "I think I'm going to like this city, firebug."

I smile back. "I think so too."

Epilogue

Beckett

Our new apartment is much warmer in the winter than the old one, but that doesn't stop my hand from shaking right now. I adjust my tie as I stare back through the mirror and watch Quinn put on her white sweater dress. It's a beautiful A-line that flares out and sways around her.

She walks into her closet and comes back out a few minutes later with her engagement ring on and I smile when I see it. Our wedding bands sit heavy in my pocket as I try to take a deep breath and calm down.

I proposed to Quinn in October and I haven't been this scared since that day. We were walking in central park after I got off work one day and the leaves were falling perfectly and

I just... I couldn't wait anymore. I had been carrying around the ring since June but I had just never found the right moment. That was the right moment.

Quinn comes up behind me in the mirror and chuckles at my uneven tie. "Here, let me help you." She says, going to untie it.

I turn around to face her and smile into the beautiful eyes of my fiancee. "Are you sure you don't want to plan a wedding?" I ask her softly. "Your sister is going to be upset that we eloped."

She shakes her head. "I... I don't want to walk down the aisle without my dad." She whispers as she finishes fixing my tie, her eyes turning downcast.

We had started to plan a wedding. It was going to be next year in Vermont. We were going to have it back home with everyone, but plans change.

In mid November, Quinn's father passed away from a heart attack. She hasn't quite been the same since. With both of her parents gone and the rift between her and Bridget, we decided to stay in the city for the holidays this year.

It was Quinn's idea to get married on Christmas Day. Something about how we got together during the holidays last year and we should get married during them this year.

Things between Bridget and Quinn have been quiet, I don't know if they have talked at all since the funeral. We went back for it but we didn't stay long. Bridget kept making snide remarks at me and glaring even though Adriane kept trying to tell her to play nice. Honestly I think it was more uncomfortable for Quinn than it was for me.

"Quinn," I whisper, tilting her chin up to look at me, "I know you're upset with Bridget right now, but she's still your sister."

"Some sister," Quinn mutters, "She's been trying to get my fiance arrested for months even with you out of state."

I sigh, pulling her into my arms. "She's just doing what she thinks is right. Her morals are a little more strict than ours."

"I feel bad for Adriane." Quinn says into my chest, "Having to listen to my sister bitch night and day, I only have to listen to her when I call. Since she never calls me."

I walk her out to the bedroom and we sit down on the edge of our ornate king sized bed.

The headboard is a swirl of metal all of which is very good for handcuffing Quinn too. We were able to size up from her queen bed when we moved.

"What about Adriane, then?" I ask her. "Don't you think she'll want to see us get married?" Over the past year most of the communication with her family had started going through Adriane. Quinn went from complaining about her every time they talked, to telling me about the baby, to slowly calling Adriane a friend.

"We'll have Liam and Riley take pictures." Quinn shrugs.

We have gotten close with the two of them over the past year. Madison, Riley, and Quinn started spending more time together which meant we all started spending more time together.

Liam helped me get a job at the local fire department, he's asked for a few small favors intermittently since then and I never questioned any of them. I'm probably aiding and abetting something illegal, but at this point I'm too deep into it to ask questions. Regardless of whatever is happening there, I consider them friends plus Quinn and I needed witnesses.

"Pictures aren't the same as seeing it, bug." I tell her brushing some of the hair away from her face. "She'll be upset she missed it too."

"She'll forgive me." Quinn whispers. "I... I don't want a big wedding, Beck. I want to just go down to the courthouse." She walks back into the bathroom and comes out a few moments later with her boots and coat on. "We need to go, Riley and Liam are probably waiting for us."

Quinn is wearing the brightest smile as we sign the papers. I scribble my signature across it next and then Liam and Riley. We pass the papers to the clerk who very unenthusiastically says, "Congratulations." She takes the papers away and hands us our copy. "I'll get these filed. You're free to go."

We push up from the table and Quinn pulls me into a kiss. "We just got married, *husband*." She purrs between kisses.

"Yes we did, *wife*." I reply back.

Liam and Riley are wishing us congratulations as well, but Quinn is quickly pulling me away towards the bathrooms. There is one family restroom with a men's room to the left and a women's room to the right.

Quinn knocks on the door to the single bathroom and when no one answers she yanks it open and drags me inside. The second the door closes I push her up against it. It rattles behind her as my lips crush against her.

I start hiking up her skirt and the second my hands graze her pussy I realize she's not wearing panties. I pull my hands back to my pants and start undoing my slacks.

She yanks me down by my tie, tilting her head to the side to kiss me. Quinn's hands go to my pants the moment my cock is out and she starts rubbing me. She launches herself into my arms. "Fuck me." She says far to fucking loud considering we are in a public bathroom.

I clamp a hand down over her mouth and shush her. "Are you trying to get caught, firebug?" I ask and I can see the smirk in her eyes.

"Maybe." She purrs into my hand.

My jaw tenses as I look down at her. "You're going to be the death of me." I mutter as I pick her up and take her over to one of the other walls so we aren't banging up against the door.

I slide her down onto my cock and Quinn moans. "Bite it down, slut." I growl softly at her. "I don't want to find out what we'd owe Liam if he had to bail us out of jail."

She chuckles softly but nods.

I start to bounce her up and down on my cock. Her hands play with my tie intermittently pulling me down to her lips. "Quinn." I whisper softly.

"Beck." She whispers back. Her legs are wrapped tightly around me as she presses her lips back to mine. Our tongues dance around each other as she keeps moaning, "Husband." Into my mouth.

I'm about to start touching her when a loud knock sounds on the door. I'm sure we've been caught by some kind of security but then I hear Liam and let out a breath. "If we can hear you, others can too." He calls through the door. "Take it home if you can't keep it down."

"He's probably right." Quinn mutters.

I pull her off of me and set her back down on the floor. "Then let's get you back home, there I can make you scream as loud as I fucking want." I nip at her ear and she chuckles. I put my cock back into my pants, zipping back up, and open the door.

Liam nods at us as he pulls Riley into the bathroom.

"So we can't be quiet but you can?" Quinn huffs.

Liam just smiles. "Merry Christmas, Quinn."

She groans as he shuts the door in her face. I pull her down the hallway towards the exit more than a little excited to get my wife back home. My wife. I smile at her as we walk out onto the street about to grab a taxi.

The snow falls down around us heavily and the streets are quieter than usual for the holidays. Everything is peaceful even in the middle of the day which is far from normal in this city.

I take her hand and spin her softly. We start to dance in front of the courthouse in the falling snow. I take a few steps with her and then spin her again, her hair swaying around her beautifully as she twirls in her dress.

As it hits the ground, the snow melts into the salt, but I still know it was there. I still remember its impact and the way it danced before Quinn's face before fading into oblivion. And I will dance with Quinn for as long as I can before I do the same.

"Merry Christmas, Quinn." I smile at her.

She smiles back and it's the best sight of my life. "Merry Christmas."

Acknowledgements

Thank you to you, the reader! I'm always grateful for anyone who picks up my books let alone finishes them so thank you so much!

Thank you to all of my friends who celebrated Christmas in July with me while I was writing this book. I straight up decorated my office for Christmas. Something something method acting, don't judge me. XD

Thank you to my family who have put me in the position to write as much as I do. I'm grateful to be able to have the time I have to write and I just keep hoping it will go somewhere. You never know but at least having the time to try is giving me it's best shot.

Thank you to my husband who is always there for me and makes sure I stay on track. He keeps me grounded and for that I'm eternally thankful.

Thank you to all my alpha/beta readers as well as my PA (Halla) between all of your help I was able to put this book together and make it what I wanted it to be. I'm so thankful to have you all in my life.

Thank you to Quinn for surviving the worst and living to tell the tale.

Beckett, fuck you. Why you torturing Quinn so hard? Whatever, okay, thanks I guess for letting me tell your story.

Thank you to all the authors who came before me and inspired my works. Nothing is ever original and I'm okay with that. Where have I heard that before?

As always, thank you to typos. Withoot you I would be nothing. You make me the author I am today and I love you.

Finally, I want to thank God, because God gave me this book, and I feel God in this Chili's tonight.

About the Author

I'm bad at talking about myself but can write a 500 page book about someone else. Do with that information what you will.

As a kid I dreamed of being an author. I took a creative writing class in high school then proceeded to go on with my life and do nothing with it. That was until one day I decided to open a silly little document and start writing a silly little story about a healer and two kings who were in love with her. That cute little pet project that I thought would just be scrapped ten chapters in turned into a full blown trilogy that I'm more proud of than I can even explain.

I've always been a dreamer and sometimes if you keep your head in the clouds long enough, you do actually touch the stars.

I got married in September of 2024 to my loving husband. We had been together 4 years at that point and he's always encouraged me to go after what I'm passionate in. Finding that person who helps you achieve is so important and it's the best quality trait I could ask for in a partner.

Thanks for spending your time to read this. I hope you're having a great day and please make sure to check out my works. There's always more coming out. I'm one of those people who always has to be working on something so I promise you I am.

Check Out My Other Works

<u>The Asher Series</u>
    Asher
    Burned
    Change

<u>A Literal Series Name</u>
A Cozy Airport Read
A Dark Romance Christmas

The Words We Put on Our Tombstones

Check Out My Socials

Tiktok: @84Lele
   Instagram: @the84Lele
   Twitter: @84Lele84Lele
   YouTube: @84Lele

www.ingramcontent.com/pod-product-compliance
Lightning Source LLC
Chambersburg PA
CBHW021138310726
48971CB00002B/381